D0866479

Horacio Vázquez Rial

Triste's History

translated by Jo Labanyi

readers international

For José Luis Elorriaga,
who knew the south beyond the south.

The title of this book in Spanish is. *Historia del Triste*, first published in Barcelona in 1987 by Ediciones Destino.
© Horacio Vázquez Rial and Ediciones Destino, S.A. 1987

First published in English by Readers International Inc, Columbia Louisiana and Readers International, London. Editorial inquiries to the London office at 8 Strathray Gardens, London NW3 4NY England. US/Canadian inquiries to the Subscriber Service Department, P.O. Box 959, Columbia LA 71418-0959 USA.

Cover illustration by Argentinian artist Miguel Alfredo D'Arienzo
Cover design by Jan Brychta
Printed and bound in Malta by Interprint Limited

Library of Congress Catalog Card Number : 89-64271
British Library Cataloguing in Publication Data
Vázquez Rial, Horacio. *1947-*
Triste's History.
I. Title II. Historia del Triste. *English*
863

ISBN 0-930523-71-7 Hardcover
ISBN 0-930523-72-5 Paperback

Contents

Author's Prologue

I was born in Buenos Aires in 1947. In the Galician Centre Clinic. I mention this because it is no mean detail: the first entry in a biography overshadowed by what one's identity papers term dual nationality, which for me has meant a dual love, a dual anguish, a dual battle and, above all, a virtually irremediable sense of estrangement, an obsession with the enigma of identity that has marked the bulk of my intellectual output.

My first three novels - *Segundas personas, El viaje español* and *Oscuras materias de la luz* - focus on the problem of exile and statelessness from various angles. The first deals with the mass exodus from Argentina that took place in the 1970s. The second tells the story of the Republican exiles who left Spain in 1939, and their return or that of their children on Franco's death: the most autobiographical of all my works. The third is a meditation in the form of a love story, set in no particular geographical location, on the plight of those uprooted from their original context and forced to start again somewhere else. All three texts constitute a two-pronged debate on the relationship between politics and morality, history and memory, violence and rebellion.

To complete the picture, let me add that the two novels I have published after *Triste's History* - *La libertad de Italia* and *Territorios vigilados* - have a dual setting: Buenos Aires and Barcelona; and that their protagonists are Spaniards whose early life was spent on the other side of the Atlantic. My first non-fictional work published fifteen years ago dealt with the politics of population in Latin America. The doctoral thesis I am about to present at Barcelona

v

University is a population survey of the River Plate area.

These details are included not by way of a curriculum vitae - something best left to a dust jacket - but so my readers can appreciate the extent to which *Triste's History* diverges from the geographical ambivalence of most of my work.

Cristóbal Artola, *alias* Triste, is not just a character who lives in Buenos Aires; he is by and large an image of his city, which cannot be understood without reference to those who live on its fringes, just as they cannot be understood without reference to it.

The character of Triste was conceived in response to two overlapping questions, both stemming from an acute concern with the individual's role in history: to what extent is the individual aware of the impact of his actions on the overall course of history? and how do "the others" experience history?

For me, Cristóbal Artola is utterly "other", his life follows a totally different course from mine, we have no values in common, but neither is he alien to me: he has played a crucial role in my life; facing each other on opposite sides of the street, we have taken part in the same events. When I first embarked on the novel, I was convinced the difference between us was one of lucidity, *my* lucidity; I knew I was making history, in the name of progress, and I supposed he was making history without knowing it, in the name of the opposing camp. By the time I had finished writing, things no longer seemed so clear-cut. I, for my part, ended up being much less sure of my own role, and of the alleged truths of the side for which I had opted; while Triste, for his part, turned out not to be entirely unaware of the part he had played.

There was, however, still a difference: aware that my individual actions affected the lives of others, I had chosen a particular path so as to maximize their impact on what I regarded as the common good; while Cristóbal Artola, as he became aware of the consequences of his actions, chose to reduce them to a minimum. At some point in the course of his story Triste, for reasons obscure even to himself, starts to direct all his energies to finding a way of surviving that impinges as little as possible on his fellow human beings: just one of many ways of achieving dignity.

The city - not a set of buildings, but a unique place and time; our historical moment, in short - presented us both with the same contradictions. He faced them in his own way, in accordance with the values he had inherited, based specifically on a very different concept of labour from any that I, as a highly politicized middle-class intellectual, might hold: he sold his skills to survive; whether the buyer's intentions were "honourable" was immaterial. I tried to understand his motives. It took me a long time to realize he was also trying to understand mine. Not out of altruism: to save his skin. But I was not moved by altruism either, whatever I may have thought: I was also looking for a kind of salvation. I came to that realization only by reading in between the lines of his existence, writing his story, immersing myself with all the love and hatred I could muster in the atmosphere of Buenos Aires, in the sounds brought back by the memory of Buenos Aires, its sewers, its dead, its whores, its killers.

I had learnt to contemplate the horror of death without undue fear. But the world of torture, of pain for its own sake, inflicted by man on man, was something that remained, and still remains, beyond my intellectual grasp. Cristóbal Artola, having made a profession of death, found himself up against the same impossibility. In that impasse, our paths finally converged. That, for me as for him, marked the beginning of the end. We inhabited the same city and the same labyrinth as the men who had been able to take that step. My journey took me to Spain; his, to share the fate of the thousands of victims. At all stages, we were joined by history and separated by our class origins. I thought I was putting history at the service of his class, and he was putting history at the service of mine: both of us were going against the logic of events, and were doomed to disappear. And so we did.

Cristóbal Artola must be buried somewhere on his native shores, in an unmarked grave. I shall never live in Buenos Aires again.

Horacio Vázquez Rial
December 1987

Triste's History

What can I do with this old story?
Tell it to men whose thoughts are elsewhere?
Leave it propped forgotten behind a door
like a dead man's stick?

Or pour it in a trickle of dust
on to the beating heart and lap
of a new story ...?

CONRADO NALE ROXLO, *Secret*

Book I
Another South

Meanstreets
that marked my life
like the hand
of a bitter fate.

ALFREDO LEPERA,
Meanstreets

Chapter l. Triste Makes His Entrance

Regret for things now past,
sands life blew far and wide,
sadness of streets that have changed,
bitter taste of the dream that died.
HOMERO MANZI, *The South*

on its northern, eastern and every flank except for the one
that trails off into the *pampa* like a grubby, ragged strip of
lace spattered with settlements and hamlets, the city looks
out on to the mighty, open river with its one discernible
shore and its ominous yellow waters beyond which may lie
the world or nothing; solitary, sprawling, vast amid the
vastness, Buenos Aires is the south, the meeting point of
certain unmemorable destinies, of certain irrevocable
encounters, where murderous and other devious assignments
are hatched and sometimes dispatched under the shady
auspices of smalltime political bosses, born of the murky
grey of the concrete buildings and the pigeons

           - which scavenge
in the smog dotted with the twisted hands of little old ladies
reduced by loneliness to scattering crumbs that are not
exactly leftovers, vainly sowing the tarmac and paving stones
with a few dozen seeds disputed by hundreds of flapping
wings hovering without ever settling on the ground -

              Buenos Aires
is the south: in the south beyond the south, beyond the
fictitious limits of what properly constitutes the capital's
urban sprawl, in a zone thick with silence and with shabby,
ramshackle houses once upon a time set in their own
grounds and now, in 1942, swallowed up by a rash of flimsy
modern blocks and the modest beginnings of what in ten or
twenty years' time would become a swarming shanty town:

there, in the depths of a rambling one-storey slum dwelling turned by a time-honoured chain of letting and sub-letting agreements into a tenement: there, in the last of the dozen rooms occupied by a dozen families and assorted groupings, with shared use of the one bathroom without hot water and a stove with three coal-fired burners: there, in that unsavoury hole, early one ice-cold morning, Cristóbal Artola was born, the son of a washerwoman with a face bordering on the beautiful whose surname he inherited, and a passing pimp who offered to launch her under his expert protection and, on getting no for an answer, left her pregnant never to be seen again: Cristóbal Artola, known from birth as "Triste", an epithet much like those charitably applied to minor monarchs to exonerate their incompetence or feeble-ness, in this case too a cover for an inadmissibly worse predicament: for Triste was never really sad: it was more a matter of feeling nothing, of relating to nothing around him whether great or small, an indifference to all things human and divine that suggested causes more tragic, a being locked up inside himself: he was never sad or even sorry for himself, and if anything ever bound him to anyone it was precisely disaffection, if not fear or some baser emotion: just as hunger, the constant battle against hunger, decided who he threw his lot in with, carved him out a destiny, marked him with the scars that no doubt traced the figure of what would be his death

the fight for life, the fight to become a different person, to achieve cleanness, sunlight, the glow of those born to eat regular meals and lead a carefree existence, the fight for cleanness, sunlight, the glow of the well-fed, the fight for life, the furious attempt to wrench his body, his mind, away from those haunts, to get that dereliction out of sight, out of reach, tangled him in a web of desperate thoughts, of feelings of futility and impotence, of eternal exclusion in a world that seemed bent on barring all newcomers from its balmy heights but which was all too ready to add to the pile of wretches and wretchedness in its fetid depths: from the start Triste knew he was up against a stone wall whose polished surface made it impossible even to sink his teeth and claws into it, to cut himself on it while hauling himself up just a few inches, to clutch at the trouser legs of those immediately above: from the start he knew he had to adjust to the demands of the mire and learn to live in it with no hope of reward for his pains, no hope of messianic salvation such as his mother dreamt of with her pious collection of prints of San Cayetano, the Virgin of Luján and Ceferino Namuncurá, an Indian whose elevation to the company of the blessed had not saved him from an irrepressible tradition of malicious jokes about his supposed or actual homosexuality that probably dated back to the start of the beatification process: "what on earth did she collect all this junk for?" Triste would ask as he cleared the place out, still a child, putting childhood behind him, on returning from the cemetery where he had left Rosario Artola in her grave: "what on earth did she collect all this junk for?" he would ask as he re-organized for his exclusive use the room he had so far shared with the woman who had brought him into this fight to the death: "what on earth did she collect all this junk for?" he would ask as he piled a cardboard box high with devotional prints and worthless charms: but that was to come much later, at the end of childhood, an end which did not mark the transition from happiness to suffering, from innocence to responsibility: an end to childhood that was just one more date in the calendar, connected with his having been left an orphan but otherwise making no noticeable difference. Childhood was just the first stage in the terrible, useless fight to change, to become another, to rise above his meagre years, his meagre strength, his lack of words, his lack of love, the squalor that enveloped him, that choked him, that pinned him to the cracked tenement floor: his childhood was a terrible, useless fight to be another child; but he was who he was, Cristóbal Artola, known as Triste, and there was no way he could scrape out his insides, hollow out his shell to make room for someone who was more of a child, more loved, more perfect

fathers, parents: sometimes they are mere phantoms who live with their children for years on end and one day die leaving no memory behind, as if they had never existed: if some trick photographer were to erase their image from the family portrait, no one would notice; but Manuel Lema, the pimp who in a moment of ecstasy, depression or perhaps just professional expertise engendered Triste in Rosario Artola's womb and vanished without leaving a portrait, was never a phantom: precisely because of his absence he unintentionally - and unsuspectingly - played a decisive part in shaping the destiny of his son who, from time to time, would emerge from his apathy to ask about the man of whom he was apparently the living image: Don Lauro, the caretaker of the municipal depot where the horse-drawn dust carts were stabled at the end of each night's shift, was the first to give a straight answer to Triste's questions: "your father was a pimp," he told him one day, and Triste stared at him for a moment before returning to the fray: "OK, so that's what he did for a living - but what kind of a man was he?"; for in that environment there was nothing special about being a pimp, it said no more about a man than any other profession: so Lauro added, "a charmer, a loner, with a foul temper when he'd had one too many: is that what you wanted to know?" expecting Triste to mutter, "maybe; I guess so," and go back to his silence: but that wasn't what he wanted: what Triste wanted to know was why women had loved him to the point of being prepared to sell themselves for him, why his mother, who had resisted more than most, had nonetheless never forgotten him and had never looked at another man in all the days her son could remember: Cristóbal, not knowing what love was, wanted to know how to get it and whether it always led to unhappiness

there are children in whose minds, on whose shoulders, time rains imperceptibly in its slow earthward fall, soaking into their souls and bodies in a slight but insistent drizzle, washing away the traces of lullabies, childhood pranks, a taste for sweets; and under its gentle pitter-patter such children enter adolescence, another gradual transition which ideally prepares them for adulthood or, less ideally, leads them unexpectedly off the straight and narrow, away from their human origins, turning them into something else, a nightmare vision, a drunken hallucination, a deranged obsession, an object of derision
and

there are children on whom time comes crashing down mercilessly, forcing on them an age intolerably ahead of their years, out of keeping with their physical strength and appearance, beyond the grasp of their shrill, stammering voices: an in-built imbalance between the calendar, a slow growth rate and an often deficient diet transforms them as if at the wave of a wand into precocious bullies or juvenile delinquents, if not into fodder for the basest adult appetites - begging or pimping, not to mention the squalor of prostitution in public lavatories - before their frail physical frame permits: for Triste things were not so bad as for the little blind girls of five or six who in Moroccan bordellos are for a pittance forced - and accustomed - to suck the not always erect organs of affluent foreign tourists; nor were things so bad as for the young boys who in the last century spent much of their brief lives up the chimneys of Manchester's factories; or those black, yellow, red or bilious green babies who starve to death after days of waiting, swaddled in undernourished stupor, for a hypothetical plate of boiled rice which if it materializes will come too late;
but nonetheless Triste was till the age of twelve or fifteen a victim of youth and deprivation: with the onset of adoles-

cence things seemed to get a bit less desperate, but to reach that point he had to live off his wits, going to all lengths to get enough to eat, to the extent that he managed to emerge apparently unscathed but deep down marked by a trail of humiliations, insults and indelible wounds that would never leave him, not even when he had realized some of his dreams of revenge

(the dreams of those who have been badly damaged are always dreams of revenge, not dreams of justice: those who suffer the humiliations of poverty do not have the education, intellectual ability, nourishment - or class consciousness - that makes it possible for the more enlightened products of the ruling classes, in moments of insight, to formulate an objective assessment, a dream of justice, to grasp the fundamental equation between their own belief in fair play and the collective thirst for vengeance of those who are the moving force of history

- would anyone in this context dare talk of development, of the forward march of progress? -

it is true that Triste had, or thought he had, his opportunities for revenge - in each case, petty personal reprisals exacted in lieu of the long-awaited universal day of reckoning - and that he got his own back, or thought he did, time and time again, without for all that securing any of the expected improvements to his daily, and nightly, grind)

(when everything came to an end, he realized how meaningless most of his acts had been, but he also came to appreciate the important - and almost invariably tragic - effects they had had on the lives of others, on the lives of those who had meant nothing to him, for whom he had never spared a thought at the moment of committing the crimes he was ordered to commit, the crimes for which he was handsomely paid)

Triste never had any special merits: anyone in his place - and there were, and are, many of them - would have done what he did and maybe more - they might have got where he failed to get, where he was not bold enough to tread - and the overall course of history would have been no different: from his earliest years, spent in the noisy loneliness of the room shared with his mother and the noisy loneliness of the streets he tirelessly scoured in search of some supplement - in reality essential - to the precarious family diet, he realized that the many young boys in his position were interchangeable and could take one another's place in the scavenging for leftover fruit and vegetables dumped outside the market, or the snatching of a piece of meat from the bag of some housewife who, despite being able to afford it, puts it at risk by plunging into the crowd attracted by some cut-price tomatoes, or the rush on all fours past the ticket office window in the first of many manoeuvres required to get to Buenos Aires, to the centre of Buenos Aires, without buying a ticket; and finally any one of them could stand in for the other in their family lives (for want of a better term), given their markedly similar function as bread-winners for their various dependents: such differences as existed between Triste and his peers, and between them in turn, were a mere matter of technique: while one would limit himself to snatching accessible objects protruding from baskets and shopping bags, another would slash the side with a knife and make off with the best pickings, while yet another would go for cash rather than kind, deriving his earnings from unattended purses or unfastened handbags: Cristóbal Artola, with his sad, expressionless face, carried a knife in his pocket from the age of six, an inoffensive-looking knife with a stubby blade, which on the day of his mother's death he swapped for a bigger one with a fearsome blade and spring: an efficient tool with which he marked the hand of the first greengrocer who caught him in the act and made the mistake of shouting "stop thief!": Triste turned on him, with the two stolen oranges in the canvas bag he always carried slung over his left shoulder, looked him in the eye and spat in his face:

when the man made as if to raise his arm, whether to wipe his face or hit out is not clear, he found his movement blocked by the knife in the boy's right hand: he simply held the knife steady and let the man cut his own hand, the energy of the gesture determining the depth of the wound: moments like that were Triste's trademark: in such things he was, and always had been, unsurpassed

his was not a childhood, but he survived and learnt to survive: if he had made it to the age of ten, eleven, thirteen, he could go on making it to a reasonable age: the world about him was not changing and with every passing day he was gaining in strength, in assertiveness, making more of a name for himself, becoming more of a real man

Chapter 2. The White Doll

dead of night amid the blazing candles
oh burning heart broken to bits
scattered like fires or furies
JUAN GELMAN,
lament for the feet of andrew sinclair

the embalmer got down to work within a few hours of the
sad demise - it was "at 20 hours 25 minutes", as all the
national radio stations would repeat every night for the next
few years, that after a long struggle, "Eva Perón, the
spiritual leader of the nation, became immortal" - as soon as
he had been able to get the basic equipment together and
procure an assistant; Pedro Ara, summoned by the
deceased's husband, never divulged the details of that night's
work: a huge gap, filled with clichéd reflections on the
subject of death, exists in his memoirs between the moment
when he writes, "Perón and I went into the funeral chapel
together," and the subsequent mention of dawn coming up
over the River Plate, the latter being the sole statement of
fact found before the phrase, "the body was now absolutely
and definitively incorruptible": the morning ushered in by
such extraordinary goings on was that of the 27th July 1952:
in the course of that day the body, conserved but not yet
fully embalmed, was laid out in a reception room in the
Ministry of Labour and Planning, where arrangements had
been made for it to be displayed, for whatever period of time
might be deemed necessary, to the devotion, adoration,
comment or curiosity of the people, strictly controlled by
rows of soldiers and uniformed police lining both sides of a
narrow corridor which reduced to a narrow trickle the
hundred-thousand-strong crowd who, over the next sixteen
days, made the pilgrimage to pay it their last respects: that

initial homage to the deceased was accompanied by endless torchlight processions: the same gloomy processions, reminiscent of Holy Week, would be repeated a month later and on each of the three anniversaries of the death celebrated before the widowed President/General's fall from power in 1955: the three anniversaries celebrated with the immaculate body laid out on the second floor of the General Workers' Confederation headquarters, till the night of the 23-24th November 1955, when it would be loaded into a military truck bound for some unknown destination, vanishing off the face of the earth till - no other reliable mention exists - the 4th September 1971, when José López Rega, in his capacity as Perón's personal secretary, summoned Dr. Ara to inspect his handiwork, the date and manner of whose arrival at Perón's Madrid residence-in-exile remain shrouded in mist

thanks to the fervour and determination of Rosario Artola, her son Cristóbal, who had just turned ten, did not sleep on the night of the 26-27th July 1952 nor for much of the following night of the 27-28th, when they found a place in the sequence of events that allowed them to achieve the goal of such prolonged abnormality: almost 48 hours staving off hunger and fatigue, through the various shades of daytime grey and the night-time black offset by the damp, anaemic glow of the endless flares somehow resisting the persistent drizzle, would have been too much for another child, but Triste stood impassively and uncomplainingly at his mother's side, clutching her tightly clenched hand, observing rather than hearing the prayers muttered by virtually the whole crowd pressing round the Ministry building, blurring into a single drone whose pious zeal contrasted pitifully with its lack of genuine religiosity: 48 hours of endurance and respectful silence, relieved only by the generous donation of sandwiches by members of the Foundation established and run till the last by the now-recumbent First Lady, sandwiches clearly insufficient for the multitudes but distributed in the best comradely spirit with the set phrase, "hungry, compañero?", which in Triste's case was met by an unambiguous outstretched hand, with not so much as a pretence of a thank you, and in his mother's case by a plaintive, "no, compañera, how can I feel hungry when Evita's leaving us...?": for the first few hours, from dawn to dusk of the 26th, were taken up with supplications to the Virgin to intercede to save the self-styled "Champion of the Poor", giving way in the hours immediately before and after the actual death to suspense and nervous tension, and in the hours following the official announcement to outbursts of grief and a confused sense of loss and betrayal; all stages however were marked by the conviction that the end had come and that it had come before its time

in the course of the sixteen unbroken days for which the lying in state lasted, Buenos Aires was flooded by men, women, children, people of incredible age and hitherto unsuspected races: specially chartered coaches transported them from the four corners of the Republic, from places whose names - given the uninspired nature of most of the country's place names - sounded strange to the ears of the capital's inhabitants, places to which the radio or some casual visitor had nonetheless carried the First Lady's fame: thousands - tens and hundreds of thousands - of free train tickets were given away so no one would miss the posthumous apotheosis: as they got to the unimaginable city, they were pointed in the direction of the Ministry where the funeral chapel was installed, and off they went to join the endless queue and wait their turn in the wintry air for hours and days on end: many of them came from places where they had next to nothing or nothing at all: tumble-down shacks and food when it could be found: many took the opportunity to make the journey they would otherwise never have been able to make: the journey that gave them the chance to put behind them their state of neglect, to start a new life that was more like being alive, no matter how monstrous, hostile and unrelenting Buenos Aires might be: many of them stayed for good: once the statutory visit was over, they set off in search of some relatively unpopulated or built-up area where they could reproduce an urban version of the hovels they had left behind them: many coaches went back to their distant provinces empty and there was a glut of free railway tickets for a return journey indefinitely postponable and postponed: many of them found what they took to be a suitable environment in the south beyond the south, in the slums where Triste eked out his days learning the art of growing up; and in its rubble and mud, with four wooden stakes found on some rubbish dump and a few sheets of rusty corrugated iron, they constructed the makeshift shacks to which they would cling through life and death for the next ten, twenty, thirty years, resisting police harassment, army raids and all the endemic evils of a universe without drinking water, electricity or facilities of any kind. Standing in the persistent drizzle, Triste saw the first to arrive, those from the relatively nearby centres - or margins - of habitation who had travelled a mere two or three hundred miles: afterwards, almost immediately afterwards, he would see them set themselves up round the house where he lived, patiently, silently fetching and carrying the magically procured materials that would become their homes, taking on a host of heterogeneous identities, bent on conforming to the requirements of the situation: skivvies, waiters in seedy bars and taverns, servants, unskilled metal workers, building labourers, prostitutes, dockers in the case of the fittest: those whom Triste watched arrive in those early hours were soon joined by thousands more: relatives brought from the provinces with the hard-earned or ill-gotten pesos sent home by the advance guard, the last to benefit from the late Evita and the chance concurrence of an offer of free transport: and with the relatives came friends, neighbours, acquaintances, all lured by the same dream of making it in the city: that day, and in the days immediately following, if not for the whole of the sixteen days during which the body was laid out, they stood resolutely waiting to pay their modest respects and get a distant glimpse of the lovely face asleep under the oval glass panel in the lid of the coffin, sustained only by the odd item of food distributed by the ladies of the Evita Perón Foundation: "hungry, compañero?": "yes, thank you, compañera": unaware of being in what was perhaps the only nation left on earth in which the giving and receiving of alms retained the honourable, non-humiliating status it had enjoyed in the Middle Ages

on his knees throughout the evening of the 26th July, never letting go of his mother's clenched hand, registering her grief through the tightening or relaxing of her grip: on his knees throughout the evening, not knowing how to join in the prayers because no one had ever taught him and all he could do was try to mimic other people's gestures and movements with no understanding of the inner postures - of thought, feeling or spirit - to which they corresponded: on their exhausted return to the one shared room, Triste asked, "how do you pray?" and listened carefully as his mother recited two or three Pater Nosters and Ave Marias, convinced he would remember the words for the rest of his life, so great had been his need of prayers the day before: after his mother's third repetition of the sacred formulae, believing himself now to be in possession of the keys to the divine bureaucracy, he said, "that's enough," and lapsed back into his usual silence: Rosario never found out whether her son had really learnt how to say his prayers properly because the first time he prayed out loud was two years later, over her remains, bidding them farewell

on his knees throughout the evening of the 26th July: on his feet throughout the night, the news of the outcome having been released, periodically holding lighted torches which kept being passed to them and which they in turn passed on to some empty-handed bystander: watching the ever longer columns of people of all ages and stations wending their way, torches aloft, to the Ministry building housing the illustrious corpse and its preserver: only on the morning of the 27th were those who had been queuing up for hours allowed to enter the funeral chapel, in single file, in order to linger for a moment over the coffin, briefly admiring the object of their hopes or love or hatred, sighing, sobbing, praying or letting out a shriek and fainting on the spot, an eventuality foreseen by the organisers and instantly taken care of by a troupe of robust uniformed nurses who swept the victims up, carried them off to a consulting room curtained off from public view, brought them round and sent them out into the big wide world by a different exit

Triste and Rosario were among the first to arrive but that did not give them much of an advantage when it came to lining up in a queue and embarking on the seemingly unending shuffle forwards: it was not till the early hours of the 28th that they got to the room where the impassive, improbable, invincible corpse, eternalized by the elimination of all likely sources of bodily corruption, was laid out for public display: finally they entered the room: sandwiched between those ahead of them in the queue who insisted on spending longer over the bier than was strictly necessary to get a look and mutter a quick prayer, and those behind pushing, like them, in their eagerness to get their share of the funereal spectacle before their energies failed them, they went in through the door: in the distance, inconceivably distant, they saw her, a magnificent white wax doll beneath a glass panel, a white doll cosmetically embellished inside and out, with an overdone theatricality, especially for the occasion, an occasion that would be repeated to exhaustion point for millions of people like Rosario and Triste, the perfect send-off for a great star who had been no such thing, the moment of splendour which had perhaps been dreamed of by the second-rate bit-part actress which is what she had been: they went in: they saw her: Triste, still clutching his mother's hand which was sweating and more tightly clenched than ever, did not really know what he was doing there, apart from submitting to the authority of the woman who had brought him into this world and who, at the sight of that white doll, dissolved into a torrent of tears the like of which he had never seen her shed for anything or anyone: he remained unable to grasp the meaning of that visit, unable to comprehend his mother's faith in so many things - prints, charms, words - that seemed to him futile: they went in: Triste saw her, he saw the painted white doll lying in what was supposed to be her final resting-place: he was never able to understand why he never forgot her, why her image flashed before his eyes at the moment of his own death: just as he was unable to understand, till faced with the prospect of his brief existence coming to an end, how all that waiting in the rain, that so brief filing past the body, that so slow journey home exhausted and starving, how all those acts and gestures were political acts and gestures: it would cost him so much, he would have to go through so much to find out: to realize that those acts and gestures, like so many others in his subsequent career as hired assassin, pimp, bodyguard, were political acts and gestures: it would cost him so much to find out, to realize that he was destined for politics and that his destiny had been fulfilled beyond his wildest dreams, wishes, or fantasies: it would cost him his life

Chapter 3. Ghosts in the Night

In Santa Cruz, between the hills and the sea,
I have seen the little cemetery of the shot strikers.
RAUL GONZALEZ TUÑON, *Patagonian Cemetery*

in a totalitarian regime like that of the celebrated People's
General, the only possible strikes that can take place are
those ordered by the Government to put the screws on
certain private citizens whose loyalty is more or less suspect
and whose position can be more or less impaired without
jeopardising the system: so when something as unusual as a
non-government (indeed anti-government) strike takes place,
the strikers and strike-leaders are putting their heads on the
block: in the "Free, Just, Sovereign State of Argentina"
proclaimed by the official propagandists and ruled by the
twice-elected comrade-in-arms of Mussolini, in which the
trade unions and workers represented by them had no choice
but to be Peronists and could down tools only on a day
officially decreed as being in honour of Perón - "let the
bosses do the work" was one of the slogans chanted by the
party faithful - the unthinkable happened: the leaders of an
unlikely organization representing the train drivers - only
the train drivers: not the railway workers as such, who
belonged to the Peronist Railway Workers' Union - and
known by the name "Fraternity", a name with anarchist
connotations despite the fact that it had long ceased to have
anything to do with anarchism or socialism or communism, a
fringe organization now largely forgotten and chiefly made
up of Radical Party sympathisers - no longer particularly
radical - in an extraordinary move took it upon themselves
to paralyze the nation which depended for its livelihood on

the export of beef and wheat from its vast hinterland, by the simple expedient of refusing to run the trains

- later (or perhaps earlier, in a country with such a bad memory it makes little difference) the rubbish collectors of the noble city of Santa María de los Buenos Aires almost buried under a mountain of garbage the achievements claimed by nearly a decade of posters, broadcast speeches, florid eloquence and the universal presence of the Presidential Couple (originally) and Widowed President (subsequently), forcing the latter to dismount from the steed on which he was always pictured in the equally universal photographs, and sit down at the negotiating table; but that's another story: the emissaries of municipal hygiene were not a major feature of the slums where Triste lived -

the fury in high places at the audacity of a tiny handful of workers in presuming to take on the First Worker and his millions of supporters led to the immediate bringing in of the army to get the trains running - with the ensuing casualties - and the equally immediate arrest of several of the publicly known leaders of such an outrage

after the necessary interventions, violent reprisals against the striking workers and negotiations that were bilateral in name only, coal once again began to be shovelled into the locomotives, the more modern diesel engines were once again started up, and everything returned to normal: the press dropped the subject - not that it had ever said much about it - and the fate of those initially arrested was never known: malicious tongues and the usual irrepressible, unofficial grapevine put abroad the most extravagant, terrible, blood-curdling rumours: that they had been deported to the penal colony of Ushuaia, in the south; that they had been taken to the north and abandoned in the jungle; that they had had their tongues ripped out under torture to silence them for ever; that they had been tied to the tracks and run over by the first train to go back into service, on a siding outside an isolated village in the middle of the *pampa*: but of all these rumours, of all these unconfirmed eports, the most persistent, prevalent and plausible affirmed that they had been snatched from the secret police by men in army uniform and shot at dusk on the third day of strike action; such a rumour would never have reached Triste in the troubled year of 1953 had it not been for the unfortunate experience of one of Rosario's neighbours who, on the said date, decided to visit the grave of her late husband in La Chacarita cemetery

like the Parisian cemetery of Père Lachaise where, even in the present trough of Gallic decadence and materialism, someone, some anonymous person from some corner of the city or of the globe, will always remember to put flowers on the graves of Edith Piaf or the occultist Alan Kardek, so in La Chacarita cemetery in Buenos Aires there is always some offering on the tombs of Carlos Gardel and Mother María: Doña Amanda, Rosario's neighbour and confidant, on the way to her regular post-matrimonial tryst, stopped off to leave some carnations at the foot of the monument to the popular healer, whereupon it seems she became so engrossed in thought that she lost track of the hours: what with the time spent on such personal obligations and the long walk through the vast necropolis to reach the mortal remains of her poor Victoriano, dead and cremated some ten years now and housed in one of the so-called "integral pantheons" - long, forbidding, multi-storey rows of identical, almost anonymous niches covered with stone slabs, indistinguishable from one another except for a barely legible name or number inscribed on a bare metal plaque - where she intended to place some lilies in the horizontal metal ring with which her late husband's last abode was equipped: what with one thing and the other, plus an inability to concentrate owing to the unusually profound thoughts on her mind - her normal inclination being to busy herself with tasks that left no room for strenuous intellectual or emotional effort - the hours slipped by and the tall wrought-iron cemetery gates were closed without her hearing any of the successive warnings - a sinister bell tolling insistently - normally given in such places to remind any grieving relative still remaining of the need to sleep under a roof, in a bed: when Doña Amanda realized the time, it was too late: night had fallen and it would be virtually impossible not only to find someone to let her out but even to find her way to the exit in those vast grounds

for the first three, four, five hours the poor woman - who had no notion of the existence of Edgar Allan Poe and had never heard of Hamlet or H.P. Lovecraft - was panic-stricken, unable to move an inch, afraid to call out in case the grim stone slabs surrounding her on all sides echoed her cries back at her, magnified and distorted: she was not aware of counting the twelve metallic strokes announcing midnight, but at the last stroke some mysterious, nameless inner mechanism set her in motion, steered her up the steps to the level of the individual graves - many of those densely populated pantheons were designed as sunken semi-basement areas - and sent her running wildly along the paths which she could barely make out in the moonlight between the vaults and the horizontal tombstones: on the verge of exhaustion and drenched in sweat, she came to a halt in some totally unknown place, faced with nothing but blurred shadows ahead, her primitive instincts trained on any sound or movement around her that might stand out from the constant drone of insects and the swaying of the cypresses in the wind: the scurrying of a rat or the hooting of an owl would have sent her over the brink into madness: she did not see or hear anything of the kind, but after that night she was never the same again: she saw and heard other things, was a witness to acts and faces, she overheard what was said by those who, in the middle of the night, at dead of night, came carrying their strange load: it was after the distant, impassive belltower had struck three: she had carefully counted the three strokes and was waiting for a fourth, a fifth, a sixth, for morning, as she had never longed for anything in all her life before, shaking with cold, shaking with fear, full of resentment at the widowhood that forced her into situations not of her choosing, full of a desire to go on living that made her feel waves of revulsion for those sleeping all around her, won over by the forces of destruction, by the horrors of non-existence

she had carefully counted the three strokes and was waiting for those that must surely follow when the purr of an engine, and seconds later two dipped headlights moving towards the spot where she was, punctured that spine-chilling nightmare, bringing her sharply down to earth from the supernatural plane where she was lodged: the object moving towards her, and coming to a sudden halt some fifty yards from the tombstone on which she was sitting, was a military truck, covered with a thick green tarpaulin stretched over a high, arched, metal frame: she made no attempt to hide and the truck driver spotted her well before she had woken up to the fact that something quite out of the ordinary was taking place before her eyes: out of the right-hand side of the driver's cabin jumped the man she instantly realized was in charge: he landed on the ground, shouted "all out!", and came running over to Doña Amanda who, wide-eyed, was looking on as fifteen or so young men in the same uniform as the one in charge, without any badge or distinctive feature indicating which branch of the armed forces they belonged to, piled out of the back of the vehicle: "and what do you think you're doing here, sleeping in the cemetery? are you a witch or something?": "I forgot the time, sir, and I couldn't find the way out," with the wheedling tone and deferential address of those who recognize and bow to authority: "got your papers on you?": "yes, sir," the reflex reaction of those who, even in the impenetrable darkness, even when expecting to see the devil at any moment, run blindly clutching their wallet to their breast, to their hips: Doña Amanda got out her papers and handed them to the man: "Amanda Briones: right: we can't let you go now, you've seen too much, so just stay where you are; I'll hold onto your papers and we'll deal with you later": meanwhile the others had started to unload the truck, hoisting up by the ankles and armpits first one body and then another and yet another, casually and carelessly swinging them to one side and dropping them in a pile on the ground: as they made their way to a huge pit dug in advance - I could have fallen into it in the dark, the thought flashed through Doña Amanda's mind but she instantly repulsed it - she counted the bodies as they were lugged from the truck to their final destination: thirty-four of them: thirty-four train drivers, Doña Amanda said to herself, concluding almost out loud, "they're Perón's enemies": they couldn't hear her anyway, there was no one around, they seemed to have forgotten about her, but the man in charge had her papers, her identity card, he knew her name, he'd remember where she lived, she couldn't run away: she had to wait and watch what it would have been better not to see: thirty-four corpses thudding, one after another, into the enormous grave, and then the men filling it in, shovelling earth and darkness and oblivion on to them: next day the only trace of what had happened would be a patch of newly dug earth, and someone would see to it that no subsequent graves were dug in that area for a long, long time: they finished their work: the one in charge came over to her and gave her back her papers: "here you are: you didn't see anything, did you?: I won't forget your name and if I find out you've been telling stories...": he made the appropriate threatening gesture, passing the edge of his hand across his throat in an all-too-convincing imitation of a knife: "... that'll be the end of you," he concluded: by the time they'd left, it was starting to get light, just enough for her to set off confidently in search of a way out, which nevertheless took her some time: it was midday by the time she got home and summoned her neighbour Rosario to get it all off her chest: "they're Perón's enemies": "never mind; you mustn't say a word about it, understand, Rosario? not a word": promptly falling asleep the minute she had finished her tale: her friend spread a blanket over her and went back to her own room

nonetheless Rosario Artola, in half sentences and round-about phrases, unsure if she was doing the right thing, told her son Cristóbal *alias* Triste, by now aged eleven, the story of her neighbour's adventure: she started to round off her confession with the statutory phrase, "they're Perón's enemies, who shoot workers ... Perón's enemies," but faltered at the last moment, turning her gaze away from the big, sad eyes of her son who listened to her without a word till he realized she was not going to say any more, that she had nothing left to say; and then it was his turn to speak: "Perón's enemies ... are you sure?"

Chapter 4. Dim and Distant

> Whose sorrow is that the violin sings?
> What melancholy voice,
> tired of pain,
> sobs suddenly in its strings?
> HOMERO MANZI, *Your Voice Perhaps*

in sordid back rooms of local police stations or in basements of unnamed office blocks in the city centre, certain individuals were using truncheons and others (at the forefront of modern technology) were starting to use electric shocks on members of the opposition, while in the half-light of the few candles which had been lit at nightfall, in an effort not to deplete the oxygen in the room, Rosario Artola lay dying: around her, an advance version of a wake had silently set itself up, with unctuous faces, proverbial pronouncements about fate and death, rounds of *maté* tea, coffee, gin and anisette passed from hand to hand without a murmur, not even a mouthed word of thanks: as if between them they were deciding in advance the steps to be taken in the course of the following sleepless night, for there was no doubt in anyone's mind that that day was her last in this world: even Triste, standing stiffly at the foot of the bed, did nothing that was not a dress rehearsal for the posture he would adopt some twenty-four hours later at the foot of the coffin, with a black armband hastily stitched to his torn jacket by a neighbour, and a black tie lent or given him by someone who had seen their dead off many years before: at the foot of the coffin, equipped with the statutory trappings of mourning, his lips pressed tightly closed

apart from her chattering teeth and obviously taut jaw muscles, there were no tangible signs that she was dying, let

35

alone about to die in the next few hours: but the doctor Don Matías had decided to stay the night and that was proof enough: there were rumours in the neighbourhood, probably with some foundation, that Don Matías did not have the qualifications to be a practising doctor, but the fact that he did not charge much, and more often than not did not charge at all, had won him everyone's trust: he might be a quack but he never took advantage to line his pockets at the expense of the poor: as well as a quack, Don Matías was a confirmed alcoholic, like practically all the local men, though when he was the worse for wear he had the sense, unlike others, to hold his tongue and beat a hasty retreat, and no one could ever remember him getting into a fight, even as the offended party: he sat down in the kitchen, with the basic equipment laid out in readiness, asked someone to boil some water to sterilise two syringes and four needles for intravenous injections, and started to down glass after glass of gin, without entering into conversation with any of the neighbours, listening for the slightest sound from the patient's room: towards dawn, Rosario's breathing slowed down and became more regular, and her facial muscles relaxed, softening her expression and leaving her lips parted: at five past six precisely, without any warning, she suddenly sat up in bed, sweating and dishevelled, her long hair loose, as no one had ever seen her before, and with her staring eyes fixed on some imaginary point screamed, "Manuel!" and fell back, eyes closed and panting: Don Matías put his glass down on the table covered by a dingy piece of oil cloth, picked up the covered pan in which his utensils had been sterilised and went to her bed: unhurriedly he snapped off the glass top of an ampoule he had put in his pocket, and with some pincers took out of the well-boiled water the syringe barrel and plunger, together with the appropriate needle: he filled the syringe effortlessly and made ready to give the injection: first, turning to Triste, he stated rather than asked, "they've summoned her then?": Triste nodded, pondering the fact that she had called his father's name, and Don Matías plunged the needle into a vein: after ten minutes her breathing turned into an irregular, faltering wheeze, which stopped almost immediately: "it's over," Don Matías said and deftly closed her half-open eyelids with his hand: with the aid of his left hand he folded Rosario's arms across her chest, interlocking her fingers and leaving in them the tiny medallion of the Virgin she had been clutching for the past three days: it was at that point that Triste went round to the side of the bed and, bending down, kissed his mother's lifeless brow, kissed her for the first and last time: what he had not been able to do as the child of twelve he had been a few seconds before, he did as the man of twelve he had just become

the buying of the coffin and the burial arrangements were taken care of by Don Fernando, always ready to lend a helping hand, to whom everyone in the neighbourhood owed some favour or other; Doña Amanda agreed to let her room next door be used to stack up the few items of furniture in the front room, used for communal purposes, which for reasons into which no one had ever inquired was never rented: in it the funeral chapel was set up: three wreaths of flowers arrived - "your neighbours and friends", "your son", "Celinda R. de Bermúdez", the woman in Lanús for whom the deceased had for years taken in ironing - Triste did not like to ask who had paid for the wreath with his name on it: it was a debt he was not going to be able to repay: he would find out who was responsible when the time was ripe: suddenly, without knowing how it had happened, he found himself wearing a black tie and armband, shaking hands with a long row of men and women who had poked their noses in out of curiosity, faces that were vaguely familiar, no one you could call a friend, listening to the refrain, "my deepest sympathies" uttered in the deferential tone reserved for adults, and replying with a curt nod-which could equally have meant "thank you", "it's over now" or "come in and leave me alone": the ceremony went on for half an hour, all the visitors accepted a cup of coffee or a drink and left without saying goodbye: before long the gathering was reduced to its original members, the neighbours, fellow occupants of the tenement, whereupon he took up the position at his mother's feet that he would occupy the whole night: before losing consciousness Rosario had given Don Fernando the phone number of some distant relatives, the only ones she had: he rang them from the undertaker's and told them the news: they thanked him for ringing but no relative, distant or otherwise, turned up at the house nor at the cemetery next morning

that same night, as the wake was taking its due course, in the capital's Eighth District Police Station, which served as headquarters for the Special Branch - the body instituted in 1930 for the repression and torture of political prisoners by General Uriburu's highly efficient Chief of Police, Leopoldo Lugones, son of the well-known poet of the same name who in his day had announced that the "hour of the sword" had come for America - a twenty-two-year old man lay dying as a result of excessive zeal shown in the course of carrying out his duties by Police Inspector Lombilla, the man first responsible for the use of electric torture. Without wasting a minute they called the nearest doctor, who was on duty at the Ramos Mejía Hospital over the road: the doctor came, signed the death certificate, listened to the appropriate threats and detailed descriptions of what would happen to him if he told anyone what he had seen, went back to the hospital, completed his shift, went home to fetch his wife and small children and the minimum necessary luggage, and with them crossed the River Plate: as soon as he got to Montevideo, he held a press conference and told all: the international repercussions for the regime of his denunciation were tremendous: twenty years later the son of that same doctor would be a prominent leader of the Peronist urban guerrilla movement: these remote events had no apparent effect on Triste's life: he was only twelve and a few minutes before had become an orphan: his most urgent need was to replan his life: he would reject any attempt by anyone to take him under their wing, and would make his way in the world on his own: he neither wanted nor needed charity

the funeral cortège was made up of only two cars, hired by the undertaker, and it made its way at a desperately slow crawl along the dirt tracks lined with houses that led to the local cemetery, where his mother was to have her resting place; they drove in through a side entrance, between them lifted the coffin out of the hearse and carried it to a tiny chapel where a priest with a strong Galician accent gabbled his way through the Latin and sprinkled the appropriate ablutions over the bier, which was then carried shoulder-high to the nearby grave where it would be buried: the gravediggers themselves lowered the coffin into the grave with the aid of some ropes and asked the next of kin to throw in the first handful of earth: at that point Triste, who had so far stayed in the background almost unnoticed, stepped forward, threw on to the black wood a tiny bunch of violets he had got from heaven knows where, plus the first clump of earth, while starting to recite at the top of his voice, "Our Father who art in heaven ...," obliging all the bystanders to join in with the second line, "hallowed be Thy name," and get through the rest of the prayer as best they could, many of them having forgotten their years of catechism classes and others never having had such things, so that they had to make a superhuman effort to remember what they had not learnt or to learn what they did not remember: Triste went through the prayer without faltering once, from the beginning through to the final "deliver us from evil" where everyone expected him to stop: but, without a break or dropping his voice, he went straight on:

"hail Mary, full of grace" and so on: finally, to the relief of all present, he fell silent and, without so much as a backwards glance at the grave, which he would never visit, marched to the first of the two cars waiting outside the chapel door: "let's go," he said to the driver as soon as all those who had come by car had clambered in; he allowed a friendly hand to rest warmly on his shoulder for a minute, without bothering to look up to check who was responsible for the gesture: it was of no importance: he had done what he had to do, he had even complied with the requirements of his mother's religion, and now all he wanted to do was go home to be born anew

dim and distant, the image of his mother would seldom cross his mind, though in his dreams he would frequently hear her voice calling his father's name, invoking the only being who could restore her to life when she had reached the threshold of the other world: that evening he started by putting all her clothes to one side and calling Doña Amanda: "look, why don't you take all this? use what you can and give the rest away"; before doing so, he had gone through all the hems, linings, pockets, shoes one at a time: he also went through the two purses before handing them over to the neighbour and incidentally asking her if she would like to have Caruso the canary, as he couldn't keep it: touched, the old woman accepted the offer; he turned out the various cardboard boxes: dozens and dozens of photographs of strangers his mother had never shown him and which were now pointless, since he didn't know who the faces belonged to: before throwing them out, he summoned Don Lauro, the caretaker of the municipal depot, and spread them out in front of him: "Lauro, is my father in any of these photos?": the old man looked them over carefully, one by one: "I don't recognize any of them," he finally said; "they must be people your mother knew before she came to live here": "and where did she come from, Lauro?": "no idea: nobody ever asks that kind of question here": Triste threw the photos into the trash can he had procured for the purpose: his friend Fierro would pick it up in two or three days' time with his horse-drawn cart, and would take it all off to the dump to be burnt: the photos were followed by the prints and charms ("what on earth did she collect all this junk for if she died anyway?"): it was when the big wardrobe was almost empty, with just his own scant clothing left hanging in it, and Rosario's bed dismantled and scrupulously gone over - mattress and all - ready to be carted off to its final destination together with the trash can full of sentimental relics: it was when the room was just starting to look habitable that Triste made the hoped-for discovery: the ten thousand pesos - in hundred-peso, fifty-peso, ten-peso, five-peso notes, saved up one by one, by skimping on shoes, on food, on sleep - were at the back of the bedside-table drawer, wrapped in a man's handkerchief and pinned precariously to the wood on the outside with a couple of thumb tacks: now he could start to make plans, dream new dreams; he decided to get rid of his own bedside table and keep his mother's, keep her hiding place, leave the money where it was: the next day he went to pay the funeral expenses, took fifty pesos from the remaining pile and bought himself two pairs of long, tight black trousers: it wasn't enough: a few days later he managed by haggling to get two pairs of ankle boots, with a slight heel, and two dark-coloured jackets, less tight-fitting than the trousers: he didn't want to spend any more, but he had to get some white shirts and underwear, which made a considerable dent in his fortune: his appearance mattered to him: for the first time in his life he was going to Buenos Aires on his own, to make his way in the world

Chapter 5. The Second Seal

Men of the South, the sky hung heavy
on our heads.
LEOPOLDO MARECHAL, *Heaviness of Sky*

the morning of the 16th June 1955 never entirely emerged from the night, a morning choked by long threads of night hanging from an invisible sky, floating trails secreted by a lingering darkness: the strange luminosity of the dawn mist did not give way to an ever brighter sky but retreated before thick advancing shadows till it was cut off from the world by a dense, sooty blanket: at midday the blackness thickened still further portending blindness and disaster

the first to realize something untoward, unexpected, out of the ordinary was in the offing were those parents with children at school: without any proper explanation, the appropriate authorities simply rang those who had a phone or sent messages to those who did not, telling them to come and pick up their offspring: the order had been issued at top government level and they were passing it on without knowing what exactly was going on: when, three months later, Perón fled the country leaving it in the hands of a group of fellow generals, not however elected like himself, it became a commonplace to point to the events of the preceding June as the beginning of the end; they were, of course, no such thing: what happened in June was just one more link in a long causal process that had kept indefinitely postponing the beginning of the end to some receding point in the future: Triste, who was neither a child - and certainly not a schoolchild - nor a parent, but who had his wits about him and was sensitive to every aspect of the city's unrelenting, hostile atmosphere, needing to be the first to register the slightest change of mood, spotted the tell-tale signs when he got off the train at Constitución Station: a sort of hush or lull in the noisy bustle and babble that usually filled the railway terminus: virtually everyone walking just that bit faster, as if encased in a kind of transparent, gluey substance, a nauseous fluid which nevertheless permitted them to go on breathing: many of his mates, bootblacks, paperboys, porters, early-morning prostitutes, plain-clothes policemen, missing from their usual posts: the streets through which he made his way to the centre, almost deserted: fear

he strolled casually down Calle Lima, passing the Ministry of Public Works where, under the same name, the narrow roadway turns into a side lane of the vast Avenida 9 de Julio, separated from the broad central boulevard by a string of little gardens stretching past the Obelisk to the avenue's end just after Avenida Córdoba: when he got to Avenida de Mayo, he turned left and went up it in the direction of the Congress Building: he scrutinized every corner, every bar, every barber's shop, every lottery stand, in search of a familiar face: eventually, out of the Tintorería Palamás - the only place in the whole city where you could get your clothes dry-cleaned on the spot and which disappeared when it was burned down years later - stepped the unmistakable frame of Emilio, the younger of the two Lozano brothers, inveterate breakers of the Anti-Gambling Laws, both of them capable of making or taking a bet on any bingo game, lottery or horse race, indeed on any of the virtually inexhaustible range of things a human being could conceivably bet on, from the age of the waiter in the Bar Español to the sex of the child that would be born five months later to the daughter of the manicurist at the Hotel Castelar: Emilio greeted Triste with a friendly wave, inviting him to go up to him and ask, "what the hell's going on?", perhaps just to give himself the pleasure of trotting out one of his pet phrases, proffered in a smug, offhand tone: "what the hell do you expect to be going on?: nothing's going on: nothing ever goes on in this hole, kid": but Triste knew something was going on: he carried on down the street to avoid getting into a row with Emilio, to stop him putting a bet on there being nothing going on as usual, which would in turn have obliged Triste to tell him to stuff it up his arse, thus probably spoiling his good relations with the gambler, who was always doing him little favours and giving him odd jobs that, even if negligible, helped him get on in the world, in exchange for a cut of the proceeds which Cristóbal always found reasonable: having given up hope of finding anyone who could explain what was going on, he ended up sitting down on one of the benches in Plaza del Congreso to keep an eye on the surrounding streets, dream up various devices for stabilizing or even augmenting his financial reserves, and try to fathom out the strange spectacle of emptiness around him: what Triste didn't know was that the Navy had risen against Perón and had taken over Ezeiza Airport, the Naval Mechanics' School - which in later years would acquire such notoriety - and the naval dockyards: if he had known, it would probably not have made any difference; such matters did not interest him and he was not one to change his plans or course of action on account of affairs which as far as he was concerned had absolutely nothing to do with him

at about noon, after stopping off for a capuccino and pastry in a bar in Congreso, Triste set off down Avenida de Mayo, going back the way he had come two hours before, with the intention of crossing Avenida 9 de Julio and carrying on downhill, skirting the Presidential Palace to get to Paseo Colón where he could catch a bus home, or at least part of the way home: he would come back to the centre in two or three days' time, when everything was back to normal: at some point on the way he became aware that he was not the only one going in that direction: walking with him were others wanting to know what was going on, office workers going to work despite the rarified atmosphere, and various less easily classified categories of people, including some deluded souls expecting to see the Air Force parade past the Cathedral in vindication of the slighted honour of General San Martín, as in so many cases a slight so piddling it would best have been forgotten: many of the latter had congregated in the Plaza de Mayo, unaware of the rebellion in progress and of the presence of troops from the Marines lined up ready for action behind the Casa Rosada: Triste had just reached the square at 12:45 when the sound of planes overhead made him instinctively dive for cover under one of the colonnades attached to most of the surrounding buildings, in this case that of the old colonial Cabildo, which happened to be nearest: seconds later three naval bombers started to shell the Presidential Palace and the Army Ministry, without the due concern or precision needed to prevent the simultaneous shelling of the square and surrounding streets, with the consequent surprisingly high number of civilian casualties, who had nothing whatsoever to do with the uprising

Triste darted behind the columns of the Cabildo building and took shelter in a doorway protected by a protruding semicircular arch: from that position, crouching down and flattening himself against the old wooden door, he saw it all: he saw the planes drop their bombs on the Casa Rosada, where the general in question was supposed to be, on the square, where no one was supposed to be, and on the solid, modern edifice of the Army Ministry, behind the Casa Rosada in Calle Azopardo, where the pro-Peronist High Command was supposed to be: but Perón was not in his presidential office, the square was not empty, and the High Command, fully apprised of the planned coup, were not sitting waiting in their Ministry: Triste saw a shell score a direct hit on the Presidential Palace: he saw a second shell land on a bus full of passengers and the bus veer over on its left side without quite toppling over, its doors ripped off their hinges and a formless mass of dead and injured come hurtling out, bleeding and screaming: he saw a man drenched in blood emerge from the ghastly heap and run off into Calle Balcarce: he saw another shell glance off a corner of the Treasury Building, shattering the masonry and ricocheting on to the tarmac: he saw dozens more drop on every conceivable target in sight, setting on fire a car and its occupants, ripping off the leg of a cameraman trying to film the debacle, sending out shock waves shattering hundreds of windowpanes, slicing electricity cables amid terrifying showers of sparks, hurling splinters in all directions, wounding and killing any pedestrians who happened to be in the open: it was a matter of minutes or maybe seconds, but in that brief space of time Triste witnessed almost every possible variant of sudden violent death, mutilation, innocent victims screaming in pain: when he was quite sure the planes had gone and were not about to return, he left his refuge, set off southwards down Balcarce, as if following in the footsteps of the Lazarus who had emerged from the bus, and some four hundred yards down the street found a bar whose shutter was half closed, or half open: he was thirteen years old but his brazen, assured manner, and the virile assertiveness of a voice that almost overnight had changed from a hoarse treble to an even hoarser bass, made him seem several years older: he squeezed in under the shutter without pushing it up, asking if he could come in and nodding his thanks to the terrified clients: "what happened? do you know what's going on?" they cried in unison: "I can't say I know what happened: I saw bombs dropping on the square; a real massacre; give me a gin, please": "you were there?": "yes": "and what else?": "nothing I can explain: bodies everywhere" for reasons he never tried to clarify, Triste decided to hang around the area, going from bar to bar, waiting for something else to happen: it must have been about three when, on the radio in a seedy bar in Cortada de Carabelas, he heard - could not help hearing - a broadcast message from the General Workers' Confederation, calling on the workers to assemble in the Plaza de Mayo at half past six that same evening to demonstrate their support for General Perón: he jumped up and went back to Avenida de Mayo, where he found a bar stool by a window from which he had a clear view of the roadway: by half past five, people were already starting to stream past in groups, in columns, in lorries, to keep their appointment with the General

- Triste did not know either then or later, for he hardly ever read a newspaper, that the bomb he had seen land on the Presidential Palace had hit the journalists' lobby, bringing down the ceiling but killing no one: least of all, of course, the man for whom it was supposedly destined -

at six o'clock, he walked the remaining two hundred yards to the square and made for the same place where he had taken cover a few hours before: the central door of the Cabildo, under the protruding arch: by a quarter past six, the crowd numbered thousands: that was the time of the second air raid, which was much more dramatic than the first: thirty-eight planes, whose pilots aimed at no specific target and had no compunction about killing civilians, strafed the crowd, dropping shells and firing with machine guns: a few people managed to escape miraculously by running into the adjoining streets and taking refuge in those few hallways where the doors were opened to let them in: the planes flew over the square twice and then made off into the distance, bound for the Uruguayan coast where they effectively succeeded in landing: having failed to seize power, they were going into exile till Perón's fall became an established fact: in later months no one ever called them to account - no one, that is, with the authority to call them to account and be taken seriously - for the part they had played in the massacre: indeed it was not to be Triste's last experience of such things

when the planes had disappeared out of view, the survivors fled as best they could, and the dead and wounded were left lying on the ground waiting for assistance, Triste discovered that his decision to hang around the centre and not go home early, his presence in that bloody arena, had a purpose after all: a few yards away from him, flung on to the roadway by the impact of some falling shell, limp as a puppet with its strings cut, he spotted Don Lauro, the old caretaker of the municipal depot: he ran over to him and raised his head, as he had seen people do in the movies, and, as in the movies, the injured man half-opened his eyes and recognized him: "Cristóbal: this time we're done for": "Lauro, what can I do for you?": "nothing, son, can't you see my luck's up?": they stared into one another's eyes for one or two minutes, remembering things, possibly pleasant things: Lauro smiled: "Cristóbal: that wreath with your name on it at Doña Rosario's wake, it was me that ordered it: you don't owe anyone anything now": "you mean I can't pay you now, Lauro, that's not the same": "stuff that pride of yours: you don't owe anyone anything": they both knew that the terrible wave of pain creasing the man's body, which Triste registered in his fingers supporting the man's neck, meant that death was but a short step away: "goodbye, son," Lauro said before shouting with what little strength he had left, " *Viva* Perón, godammit!" and sinking into the expected, unexpected blackness

Triste was entirely ignorant of what, a few months later, would constitute the second act of the tragedy in which, like it or not, he was condemned to play a part: the executions that took place in the town of José León Suárez, in the province of Buenos Aires, after Perón's fall from power would become known to him belatedly only several years after the event: there too men died, men like Lauro, plus a real general

Cristóbal left the square after going through Lauro's pockets - he had two hundred pesos on him and his identity card: Triste kept the money and put the identity card back - and set off for Constitución Station: on the whole way he found only two bars open: he had a gin in each of them: the train journey seemed shorter than usual: it was raining when he stepped out on to the platform and ran to catch the *colectivo*, a kind of shabby, battered bus, which would drop him off on the corner by the depot a hundred yards from the tenement: as the vehicle's lights disappeared into the distance he was left in total darkness: he went into the depot by the side entrance which was always left unlocked: there were the horses and carts: no one would go out to collect the rubbish that night: not needing a match or any other light, he made straight for the shed that had been the old man's home, closed the door behind him, and only then, knowing no one could see in from the street, lit the candle on the table: he did not have to look far: the five hundred pesos - and Cristóbal knew there couldn't be much more than that - which Lauro had scraped together were in the same drawer where he kept the two plates, two knives and two forks which served him and the odd special guest: Cristóbal pocketed the cash, snuffed out the candle and went out into the street through the little wrought-iron gate, checking for sounds or movements in the dark to make quite sure no one had seen him: it was not till the evening of the following day that he would hear people in the tenement saying it seemed Lauro had been one of the air raid victims, which meant there was no longer any cause for concern:

immediately after leaving the old man's shed, moving in the darkness as easily as in the full light of day, Triste had gone to his room, lit the candle, locked the door from the inside and tipped the seven hundred pesos he had just inherited out on to the bed: he wrapped four hundred - four notes of a hundred each - up in the handkerchief at the back of the bedside table, and distributed three hundred - six fifty-peso notes - between the small pocket inside his waistband, his right-hand trouser pocket and the inside pocket of his jacket: he then took the precaution of undoing his earlier precautions: he left the door ajar, boiled and drank some *maté* and munched his way through some stale biscuits in full view of any one who might care to look in, turning over the pages of a volume of Almafuerte's poetry, one of the five books in his possession: finally, he blew out the candle and got undressed: before climbing into bed he shouted silently, " *Viva* Perón, godammit!" thinking of Lauro, the seven hundred pesos, the blood

Chapter 6. Billiards

Little Buenos Aires café,
I sing to you and to no other,
for nothing else in all my life
has been so like a second mother...
E.S. DISCEPOLO, *Little Buenos Aires Café*

when Triste was fifteen, and looked decidedly more like a grown man of twenty, he concluded the time had come to extend his hunting-grounds to that exclusive Buenos Aires institution that is the café, the place where all the city's business, above and below board, is done or undone, the outpost of civilization in the city's none-too-civilized outskirts: the pioneers who, on the orders of Rosas first and Roca later, set about the co-ordinated extermination of the Indians sowed the infinite wonderment of the *pampa* with the primitive beginnings of that central pillar of civic life: the saloon bars, christened by the Galician immigrants who ran them with the name of "pulperías" out of nostalgia for the "pulpos" or octopi last seen on setting sail for America to seek their fortune, saw the first gambling sessions, the first interminable rounds of Dutch gin smuggled across non-existent frontiers, the first clumsy knife thrusts, the first song contests between fearless, quick-tongued *gaucho* minstrels and the Devil, the first clinching of friendships and the first betrayals: in 1957 the cafés of Buenos Aires were all that and more: somewhere to while away the time, to listen to the radio, to gamble illegally at billiards, dice or poker, to solicit and to hire assassins of any shape or size, to contract and pay debts (debts of honour, need it be said), to scribble verses on paper napkins and compose novels out of overheard snatches of conversation: the cafés of Buenos Aires were also the haunts of men of a certain notoriety: as

51

gigolos, as cardsharpers, as skilled billiard players, as unrivalled dancers, as lady-killers, or alternatively as inveterate losers whose good humour nevertheless earned them the sympathy and respect of those who in that miniature universe constituted the winners: Triste, thanks to his introduction by Emilio and Julián Lozano, familiar faces in all the late-night, or all-night, gambling joints in the city centre, and familiar faces also with the police, scored his first hit on the green baize of a café in Calle Callao, frequented by professional billiard players and by the best amateur devotees of the art: the crushing defeat he inflicted the very night of his debut on one of the most celebrated players of the day turned him into a talking point virtually overnight, attracting to that select venue certain wealthy individuals interested in witnessing and, if things went their way, backing the birth of a new champion: in the course of the first two weeks Cristóbal was watched by every connoisseur in the game: on the first day of the third week, one of the scrawny hangers-on he had got used to seeing round the table approached him and informed him that Don Marcos Peña - a smooth, stout gambling racketeer whose influence was such he had never once been arrested in the whole of his long career - wanted to talk to him as soon as he had finished his game, at one of the tables at the back of the café: Triste went over some twenty minutes later and sat down at the table without asking permission, looking the man who promised to be his salvation in the eye: "a coffee," he said when the waiter came over: "and how about a little something else?" Don Marcos offered: "I don't drink while I'm playing: I gather you want to talk to me": the man dismissed the waiter (still hovering in expectation of a further order) with an unequivocal gesture, and turned back to Cristóbal: "how much do you think a good billiard player might be worth? a player like yourself, for example": "I don't know how much he might be worth," Triste virtually confessed, "but I've a pretty good idea what he might cost:

make me an offer and then we can start talking": "right you are: seven thousand a month, as a basic wage; and five per cent of the winnings if they exceed that sum: if they come to less, you get the seven thousand anyway": "and who sees to that?": "I do, isn't my word enough?": "sure, sure; and is the player in the know?": "does he know if the bets are for or against him, you mean? he's never in the know; the police round here have got that absolutely clear, you can bank on that": "fine: when do we start?": "you already have: all tonight's games are taken care of: you've got three to go, does that suit you?": "can it not suit me?": "no": "so?": "that's it, then: here's an advance," Don Marcos rounded off, pushing an envelope over to Triste's side of the table: he slipped it unobtrusively into his inside jacket pocket, got out an American cigarette, lit it without offering one to the man, who was clearly a cigar smoker, got up and went back to the billiard table, where several inquisitive faces were already waiting for him to start: "someone here's not going to come out of this so well; too bad," he thought as he reached out for the cue

that night, when he got back to the tenement, he opened the envelope and counted five thousand-peso notes: he hesitated over whether to trust them to the handkerchief too, wondering if perhaps the time had come to think up another hiding place: partly out of inertia, but also partly because he couldn't see the point of putting his money in some other equally accessible place, he convinced himself things were best left as they were, arguing that there was nothing he could do about it till he was eighteen and old enough to open a bank account: and even then he would have to put the money aside so as not to put too much into his account at any one time, to avoid questions being asked about the source of his earnings: seven thousand a month would do for the time being: later on he'd ask for more: he fell asleep as soon as his head hit the pillow and dreamt of Don Marcos sitting at a billiard table on which were piled stacks and stacks of banknotes, in all colours and denominations

at the end of his second day as a professional, he went home with a package he'd been carrying round with him since early that day: he screwed up the newspaper wrapping and stood on the table two bottles of Bols Dutch gin, earthenware bottles like those old ladies fill with hot water to warm the bed: he put the neck of one of them in the china bowl which he used for shaving and which always had water in the bottom: he held it there till the paper seal was soaked through: then he carefully peeled it off, prised out the cork with a knife, making sure the top of it was left unmarked, filled two big glasses with gin and started to drink the first, emptying the rest of the bottle into the chamberpot and walking to the other end of the house to tip down the lavatory the contents of that nocturnal receptacle he never used, and to throw into the big communal dustbin the newspaper in which the parcel had been wrapped: the gin bottle without gin in it now being ready for use, he made sure the door was properly locked and completed the series of manoeuvres which, since getting back to the house, he had taken care to hide from public view, unpinning the money from the back of the bedside table and rolling it up tight to fit into the neck of the earthenware bottle: into its dark interior went forty thousand-peso notes, perhaps a bit the worse for wear but without Cristóbal having to exert too much pressure: finally he put the seemingly intact cork back in place and stuck the paper seal back on, so that the whole was restored to its original state: if he needed to touch the money, he'd break the improvised money-box open: in the meantime it was safer there, especially since he'd left a few pesos in the usual place, where he could get hold of them more easily, with the added advantage that they would serve as a handy decoy to stop any would-be burglar investigating further: "though no one in their right minds would break into this den of thieves," the boy thought: but when he had roughly uncorked the other bottle and placed it squarely on the table, putting the one with the money in it away in the big wardrobe that doubled as sideboard and wine-cellar, perfectly visible to anyone who might open the door, looking like part of his reserve supply, he unlocked the door and started to breathe more freely: sunk in thought, he dispatched the two generous helpings of gin he had poured out at the start, in solitary celebration of his achievements to date and to come, and flopped on to the bed, fully dressed: he woke up at around six, had a drink of water, got undressed and went back to sleep till well into the morning

three months had gone by since his first talk with Don Marcos, three months that had brought in a regular and not inconsiderable flow of earnings - the last envelope had had nine thousand pesos in it - when, at the start of the evening, the racketeer walked into the café and, without stopping to say hello to anyone present, nodded to Triste, pointing to the table at the back: the waiter hastily set two cups of coffee and two glasses of water on the table between them: "happy with the way things are going?" the older man inquired: "can't complain," came Cristóbal's laconic reply, adding: "anything bothering you?": "not exactly; but tonight you're booked to play against Riestra, Avellaneda's man, right?": "that's right": "you're to lose": a prolonged silence from both men, and then Don Marcos again: "you don't imagine I hire you to win all the time, do you?"; "no, sure, I know that's part of the deal: but Riestra gets my goat and the thought of letting him beat me ...": "look here, Triste, I've already fixed things and there's a lot of cash at stake, so just shut your mouth: you're to flunk two shots and let him take the lead; if not ...": "if not, what?": "nothing, nothing: you'll do as you're told, won't you? you're a good kid, Triste, and I wouldn't want anything to happen to you ... get the message?": "sure I get the message, fancy man: you'll get heavy with me": that was the first wrong move Cristóbal made that day: the older man, to whom no one, not even the police, had ever spoken less than politely, stared at him in disbelief: "what did you say, kid?", wanting to reassure himself: "you heard me, you're threatening me: you're not Don Marcos the gent any more, right now you're just a heavy, a stinking hood, a goon: worse than that, a big shot with no teeth and lots of cash who gets others to do his dirty work for him: if you had any guts I'd show you respect and I'd even have lost without saying a word about Riestra: but you've got no guts, all you've got is cash": Don Marcos, scarlet, unable to take his bloodshot eyes off the boy who had hurled such a tirade in his face, got up and shot out of the bar: Cristóbal paid for the coffee which he hadn't touched

he made the second wrong move that night: Riestra turned up at about ten, hung up his coat and scarf, went to the bar to have a gin and swaggered over to the billiard table: Triste raised his eyes from his game and said: "hi; we're on at ten thirty, aren't we?": "right," replied Riestra drily: "make yourself at home and take a seat, I'll be right with you": he had to be generous because he was the home player: five minutes before half past ten, Cristóbal went to the gents to have a piss and comb his hair, giving the spectators time to take up position: they were all punters or punters' agents and had a vested interest in the outcome: they followed the game keenly and fell completely silent when it became obvious Triste was going to win hands down: the victor placed his cue back on its rest, put his jacket on, went out into the street and hailed a cab: "to Constitución Station," he ordered: from there he'd get the train and go home to bed: Don Marcos' revenge could wait till tomorrow

as he turned the corner by the depot, he saw the men waiting for him: it was too late to make a run for it so he chose to offer no resistance and let himself be knocked to the ground almost immediately: but he was only expecting a thrashing, and they had something else in mind: there were four of them and between them they flung him on to the unsurfaced roadway: then two of them pinned his arms to the ground and another held his legs, as if about to crucify him: the fourth man, the toughest of the bunch and, it seemed, the one who gave the orders, finished the job off, systematically stamping on each of Triste's hands till he heard the unmistakable crunch of breaking bones: first the right hand, then the left: "that'll do, you can let him go now": Cristóbal did not utter a single moan or insult, nor shed a tear: "that's the last time you'll play billiards: so says Don Marcos Peña, got it?": all that came back was the boy's stare from where he lay on the ground, recording that face so he would never forget it: his chance would come: "let's go," said the man to the others: when they had gone, Triste had to ease himself up on to his feet without using his hands: the pain was not yet as bad as it would get later: he ran to the tenement and kicked on the door of his neighbour Fernando, the most practical of all its various inhabitants: when he opened the door, Triste showed him his hands: "get Don Matías right away, I don't know how much longer I can stand it: take the key out of my pocket and open my door, I'll wait for you there": Don Fernando rushed off for the doctor, while Cristóbal lay down on the bed: when the two men got there, they found him unconscious: Don Matías brought him round with a big glass of gin, out of the bottle on the table: "I can't fix this for you: you need to get it X-rayed and put in plaster, and they can only do that at the hospital": Triste looked at the two red lumps at the end of his arms and said: "but there'll be police on duty at the hospital": "that can be fixed": "how much?": "I'm not sure... a thousand pesos, maybe two thousand": "Fernando, pull out the drawer to that bedside table, will you? behind it there's a handkerchief with some money in it": there were four thousand pesos: "take it all, in case it's needed": they had to walk to the main road to flag down a passing car: the two men took Triste by the arms and propped him up till a car stopped, whereupon Don Matías shouted "I'm a doctor; this man's injured and we've got to get him to hospital": it took an eternity to get to Fiorito Hospital: the pain was getting worse by the minute: at last, when the radiologist had finished, the anaesthetist took over: he woke up two hours later, his hands in plaster, still in hospital: "I took the liberty of paying for an ambulance to take you home, Cristóbal; it's a bit expensive, but Matías sealed the police officer's mouth with five hundred pesos, is that OK?": "sure; when do we leave?": "right now, if you like: you've got to come back in a fortnight's time": "let's go"

it took him six months to get back the use of his hands, and a further six months of exercises after that: somehow, with the odd job here and there, and the generous support of the Lozano brothers who, regardless of Don Marcos Peña, continued to offer him their friendship, Triste managed to avoid breaking open the bottle with the money in it: it was clear that, no matter how much better his hands got, he would never again be the skilful player he had been before: he would have to start all over again, start another life, another uphill struggle: "tough luck," he said out loud, standing in the train taking him to Buenos Aires the day they took off the last bandage: "tough luck, I'll have to try again"

Chapter 7. The Man in the Trenchcoat

"Compañero, don't go; I sense
something strange and threatening
out in the street."
EVARISTO CARRIEGO, *The Wolves*

the fact that they had broken his hands, cutting off one of
the avenues the city had opened up for him, affected Triste
less than the long delay between his recovery, his return to
old friendships and haunts, and the opening up of a new
avenue to provide an outlet for his ambitions: wherever he
turned - and he was well aware of the fact - he would find a
Marcos Peña ready to squash him, to call into question the
place that day by day he was carving out for himself in the
world: it took him nearly a year to hit on a new profession
with a regular wage packet: it was to be his profession for
the rest of his life, but he didn't care about the end, only
about how to begin: it was violent work, but he'd stopped
caring about that the moment he discovered he was capable
of tolerating physical injury without a murmur, the moment
his ex-boss's hireling started to grind the heel of his shoe
into the bones of his hand, and all his efforts went into
staring him in the face, engraving his assailant's features on
his mind for ever, in the hope of getting a chance to assuage
his anger at some later date

Triste first saw the man in the café in Calle Salta which was
his usual last stopping-off point on his way back to
Constitución Station - the café where he often met the
Lozano brothers to talk for hours on end about football or
the horses, the café, in other words, where he could always
be found, where you could leave a message for him and

where the owner, Simón Castro, a Galician born in Lugo, let him have free use of the phone. The man started to frequent the place in November or December 1959: the second time they saw him, Triste and Simón exchanged a quizzical look and the Galician shrugged his shoulders before going to take his order: whisky, the same as the first time: when he came into the café at exactly the same time for the third day running, Castro greeted him a bit more casually - but not so casually as his regular customers - and, when the man left, came over to the table where Cristóbal had for the last twenty minutes been staring at the same point of his newspaper: "what's your verdict?" Triste asked, looking up: "cop or something like that," Castro replied: "and what might 'something like that' mean, Simón?": "well, I don't know, intelligence, politics, that sort of thing ... wouldn't you say?": "sure": "and each of the three times he's paid it's been with big bills ...": "and why do you think he never takes his coat off, in this heat?": "because he's got a gun, I guess": "well done, Simón! ten out of ten, because he's got a gun: and what would a guy like that be after in a place like this?": "some robber, or some commie," said Castro, demonstrating his loyalty to prevailing values: "or somebody to do a job for him," added Triste, demonstrating his loyalty to his own interests: "you could be right: maybe he's looking for somebody to do a job for him": they left the subject there as other customers started to drift in: Triste made the journey home with a feeling in his guts he hadn't had for a long time, the feeling that something had just happened, something that would have decisive consequences in the very near future: "something like that," he thought, and realized he was fantasizing about things which, if they were true, would oblige him to define his position with regard to a certain unsavoury matter he hadn't wanted to face, but which he knew was going to confront him sooner or later - the matter of the police: at the same time he realized that he didn't have much time to think it over carefully, that in a few days' time, perhaps tomorrow, the man in the trenchcoat would follow his customary greeting by asking if he could share his table and striking up a conversation which would inevitably get around to the question of work, of money: he needed to think out where he stood in advance

on the train he bumped into his neighbour Fernando, who was also going home: they spent the journey chatting idly, about how Cristóbal's hands were after the assault into which the old man had never inquired: neither he nor the doctor had expressed the slightest interest in the matter: in their view, no one was entirely on the right side of the law, and anyone might have an accident he might not want or be able to tell the police about: and Triste was no exception, indeed he was a perfect illustration of the rule: he appreciated their tact: they spent the journey chatting about this and that, matters of no real importance to either of them, and when they got to the tenement said goodnight warmly, as the good friends that they were: friends that respected each other and were ready to do each other a favour whenever called for, without questioning the other's morals or judgement: once in his room, Cristóbal spent some time meditating on his position with respect to the world in general and the powers-that-be in particular: he had never cared much for the police because he knew perfectly well the police didn't care much for him, and all his friends and acquaintances felt the same way: so if what the man in the trenchcoat was about to propose was for him to collaborate with the police, become an informer, then his reply would be a straight no: nobody, absolutely nobody was going to jail on Cristóbal Artola's account; but if it was a political matter, that was different: he hadn't forgotten that his mother had been a fervent Peronist, and that she wouldn't have approved of the way things were at present, but that was a purely sentimental issue: it was everyone's business - and perhaps his too, why not? - to see to it that things didn't get out of hand: hadn't the police existed under Perón too? indeed weren't they the same police that existed now? weren't they, now as then, facing a common enemy: Jews, communists, terrorists, queers? it was one thing to side with those who were on your side, and another to have the guts to oppose those who were everybody's enemies: because the communists, Triste told himself, are as much the enemies of the government as they are of thieves and whores and people like me who have to fight for a living: and the Jews, he went on, are filthy rich bourgeois - he wasn't too sure what the last word meant but it made him feel hot under the collar - the enemies of all of us who haven't got a cent to our name: if it was a political matter, that was different

it wasn't the next day, or the one after, or the one after that: the man in the trenchcoat came for his whisky every night, always giving everyone a courteous greeting, treating Triste just like everyone else: and yet the latter never doubted for a minute that he was the designated recruit, the object of the visits of that stranger who, one night when Simón and Cristóbal were alone in the café, picked up something the boy had said about a horse due to run at the San Isidro racetrack the following Sunday as a pretext for joining in the conversation and finally introducing himself: he said his name was Agustín Chaves - "my father was from Galicia, just like you," he said to Simón, presumably to win him over: Simón, quite impervious to such ploys, came back with the bantering riposte: "fancy that... my son was born in Argentina, just like you" - this brief genealogical summary was the only personal detail he added to his name: he gave away nothing about what he did for a living: it was a self-introduction completely devoid of curiosity, designed to make himself known and to facilitate future conversation rather than to get to know the other two: Triste muttered his own surname through gritted teeth, thinking that Señor

Chaves probably already knew everything there was to know about him: anyway, he didn't much mind coming across as the extremely reserved man he actually was, even if Chaves could see right through him: in the world he moved in it was always best to err on the side of discretion, and the same was probably true, he guessed, rightly, in the world his new associate moved in

eventually, four or five months after Chaves' first appearance at Simón's café - it must have been March or even April, because the trenchcoat was starting to have more of a purpose - Triste's expectations were fulfilled: the man turned up earlier than usual, at five or five-thirty, and happened to find Cristóbal there despite the fact he never went there except at the end of the day - a long time later, Triste would begin to wonder if he was being watched, which would have offered a more likely explanation of why they coincided at that hour; he would begin to wonder but would put the question out of his mind, having no answer: the café was busy and Chaves had to push his way to the table at the back where Triste was sitting: the latter realized this was the moment he had been waiting for, and instinctively put himself on his guard: if not, the man would merely have given him a distant nod and settled down to his whisky at the far end of the bar, by the door: but he went straight to the table at the back: "I think the two of us need to have a little talk," he said as he got to where the boy was sitting: "what about?" Triste asked defensively: "work," a single word tossed out provocatively and which went straight home: "not here, I presume," Triste checked: "of course not: I'll see you in the Café Tortoni in half an hour's time": all decided on his behalf, with no right of reply: no doubt there were already plans drawn up for him, orders that could not be challenged, a whole destiny worked out in advance: that was the end of the conversation: Chaves went back to the bar to ask Simón for a drink, letting Cristóbal leave before him he walked unhurriedly to Avenida de Mayo, turning up it to the Café Tortoni: he was too busy thinking to take notice of what was going on around him, mulling over the various considerations that had occurred to him in connection with the appointment he was about to keep: "something like that": the cops? politics? he was taken aback to discover that Chaves had got there before him: "I ordered a coffee for you too: is that OK?": "sure, sure, that's fine": "aren't you curious to know what I'm about to propose to you?": "no: a few months ago I was, but I stopped thinking about it some time ago: we were bound to end up talking at some point, weren't we?": "thanks for giving me a straight answer: the fact is, I find it difficult to come out with what I've got to put to you": "why? is it something you're ashamed of?": "if it were something to be ashamed of, I wouldn't mention it to you or anyone else," Chaves took umbrage: and Triste took the initiative: "no need to take it personally, Chaves: that won't get us anywhere: if you find it difficult to tell me why you wanted to speak to me, we'll leave it at that, and when you feel more up to it you can fix another meeting, OK?": "thanks, there's no need: we can talk about it now: have you any idea what the job might involve?": "I hope it's nothing to do with the police ...": "don't worry about the police, no one's going to ask you to grass on a friend or ... colleague, shall we say": "in that case let's get down to brass tacks: politics?": "you know, you're pretty smart for a boy of your age": "look, Chaves, I know what I need to know to stay alive: and how do you know how old I am anyway?": "I had to find out and I've got friends almost everywhere: I needed to know if you were under age: I was never fooled by your looks, you know": "I'll be eighteen in a couple of months": "I know: we can't start work till then ... it's dangerous work: you might end up in jail and if you're not a minor it'll be easier for me to get you out": "end up in jail? why? does it involve killing someone?": "don't get scared: there's no need to kill anyone just yet: all in good time ... but you've got what it takes ... after all, you survived two air raids without blinking, didn't you?": "and how do you know about that? even the police don't know about that, as far as I know": "no, the police don't know that sort of thing - we do": "and who's we, Chaves?": "that depends, it depends on circumstances, sometimes we change names ... you'll get the hang of it in time": "I don't like working without knowing who my boss is": "I'm your boss, Artola: I'm the one who'll pay you, who'll tell you what the jobs entail: no need to worry: there's plenty of cash: we, forgive me if right now I don't put you straight about who we are ..., we want to sort this country out, we want to clean the whole place up: get rid of the communists, the Jews, the socialists, the intellectuals ...": "and the Peronists?": "we have to treat them as a special category: there are Peronists who are OK, good Peronists if you like, to put it simply, and Peronists who are a different kettle of fish altogether, misguided individuals who aren't true Peronists: the good Peronists will back us; the others will end up with the communists, mark my words, I'm not exaggerating": a sigh of relief from Triste, who can now say yes to everything: "tell me about the cash, Chaves": "thirty thousand a month, plus a bonus for each job: does that sound OK? on top of that you'll get paid for the next two months, till you're eighteen: here," and he handed him the anonymous envelope, as anonymous as the one Marcos Peña had given him but not caring whether or not they were seen: he knew what he was doing, did Chaves: "you needn't be worried about having made the right choice, my friend": "I'm not: and how about you, Triste?": "I'm not either": "how about a little drink then, Triste? we've got something to drink to: and let's drop the formalities, we don't want a repeat of what happened with Peña, do we?": "you know about that too? let's have that drink: gin on the rocks for me": they said goodbye like bosom pals, with the warm handshake and "see you tomorrow" of two buddies:

twenty-four hours later, on meeting again in Simón Castro's café, they exchanged the usual formal greeting and each of them had his separate drink and read his separate newspaper as if nothing had happened

after a while, seeing the envelope with thirty thousand-peso notes arrive each month, without anything being demanded of him in return, Triste started to have doubts and suspicions and one night, ignoring the obvious risk of being followed in turn, he couldn't help rushing out of Simón's café after Chaves when the latter left: he followed him till he saw him, in the Barrio de San Telmo, disappear through a small door that was the only opening in a huge, plain wall that continued for almost a hundred yards, ending in a garden with railings round it: he waited a couple of minutes before walking past the doorway Chaves had entered and going round the corner to see what kind of a building it was: it was a church: armed with that astonishing information, he retraced his footsteps and, on getting back to the café, asked Simón: "what time do you close?": "at three, why? do you want to stay on?": "yes, tonight I'm not going home: I need to be downtown at six thirty": "I'll keep you company": "thanks a lot: you can start by making some coffee and pouring a couple of gins, it's on me": and they talked and drank their way through the night: at one point in the conversation, Triste dropped the bombshell on his friend: "hey, Castro, do you think Chaves is a cop?": "don't know, that's what I thought when he first started coming, but now I'm not so sure": "know something? I think he's a priest": "a priest?": yes, a priest": and they went on talking about other things, as if nothing had been said, but at a quarter past six, when Triste came out from washing his face in the gents at the back of the café, he accosted his friend: "Simón, forget what I said about Chaves, will you?": "did you say something about Chaves? I don't remember a thing": "keep it that way," said Triste by way of goodbye at seven o'clock he was outside the church, waiting for the first mass to get underway so the officiating priest would not see him come in: he was prepared to spend the whole day in some dark corner of the church if necessary, till such time as Chaves might appear in his flowing robes: no one noticed him slip into the right-hand aisle: he didn't have to wait for even a minute: he let his gaze wander round the collection of old women and old men who made up the early-morning congregation, before moving on to the priest saying mass: it was Chaves: Agustín Chaves, Triste thought, St. Augustine: that was how he'd think of him from now on, by that name: St. Augustine: but he wouldn't tell him that till the end: he didn't give a damn what Chaves' occupation was, but he wanted to know: was "we" the Church? he preferred to let matters rest and leave before he was noticed: so far he hadn't been followed: he wasn't followed to Constitución Station either: he went home and slept till five: at eight he was back in Simón's café: at eight fifteen Chaves came in: "St. Augustine," Triste thought, "St. Augustine, God help us!" and he nearly came out with a cackle of laughter: "tomorrow, four o'clock, in the Tortoni," the man in the trenchcoat said to him as he passed by, barely pausing, on his way to the gents, camouflaging his words with a particularly hearty clap on the shoulder: "fine: see you there then," Triste replied: he paid and went out into the street

Chapter 8. Pogrom

On the terrible wall the three
words of the death sentence leap,
behind time's back men wait anxiously
while God sleeps his godlike sleep.
CESAR TIEMPO, *Pogrom*

four o'clock, in the Tortoni: Chaves was not alone: with him
was a squarely built youth with an Indian-looking face and
blustering manner, who couldn't be much older than Triste:
the ritual introductions were made by the meeting's
convenor: "Lorenzo," he said, pointing to Cristóbal's new
partner, who stood up and held out his hand to the new
arrival, to whom Chaves gave a new name: "César": despite
his difficulties in digesting this unannounced Roman baptism, he shook the hand offered him: "pleased to meet you",
"good afternoon", and so on: they took a while to get down
to business: the so-called Lorenzo held forth at some length
on the virtues of the warrior races and declared himself to
be of "pure white blood", born in America but the untainted
offspring of European forbears, with the same conviction
with which others before him would have declared themselves pure Aryans: "born here of Spanish parents, pure
white blood, see?" he kept insisting to Triste's boredom and
flagging smile, for he could see not the slightest confirmation of such an assertion in the face or skin of its passionate
upholder: in the end he concluded that the latter was what
Chaves would go on to call "an idealist", which label would
make Triste wonder whether the cretin did the job for
money like himself or purely out of ideological conviction: it
seemed his boss had him lined up for a joint mission not
only with the bizarre Lorenzo but with several other youths
of much the same ilk: powerful physique, more or less fascist

ideas, a desperate need for self-affirmation in every possible sphere: Chaves gave them the chance to act, they did so under their own political banner - at the time in question, that of the Guardians of National Restoration - saving him from direct involvement, while he provided the two or three hitmen who would do the dirty work: Cristóbal would become aware of such machinations, as of the existence of some higher power who managed the whole show and additionally paid his wages, as the nature of Chaves' relationship with them became apparent: but the fact of the matter is he didn't come to appreciate the full scale of the operation till he was too involved for there to be any turning back: when he heard his St. Augustine say, "we're going to carry out a pogrom," he stared at him blankly: he'd never heard the word before, and his drinking companions took it upon themselves to instruct him that it meant an attack on a Jew: "any Jew?": "well.. strictly speaking, yes, but in the case of this attack we've selected a very special one, a Jew who..."

in practice, the victim turned out to be a Jew who was not the slightest bit special, a perfectly ordinary Jew, chosen as a target for reasons that had nothing to do with him but with the fact that he had a shop on the ground floor of an apartment block in Barrio Once: the pogrom was, in fact, a mere cover for much more significant events that were to take place at the same time three storeys up: the shopkeeper was simply a Jewish watchmaker who sold cut-price watches and was good at repairs: a nobody: at him were to be thrown first a tar bomb, to damage the shop's facade and make a political point, and then a bomb that would make a big bang and give off lots of smoke, to focus the attention of everyone in the area on the shop for a couple of minutes: Triste found all this out when he got there and was entrusted with throwing the two bombs: in the Café Tortoni all he was told was that, while they were carrying out their operation, another group would carry out a complementary operation in the vicinity: those were the only details he was given, crude details in every sense of the word, with a lurid and patently false caricature of the Jew that made Cristóbal feel uncomfortable: they arranged to meet up in a bar near the ordained target of attack the following day, at five in the afternoon: virtually the whole group would be there: Triste left, by now convinced the so-called Lorenzo didn't get paid a cent, after shaking his hand and that of Chaves

as they arrived one by one, Triste had no difficulty working out which of them did it for money and which for free, which were professionals and which amateurs driven by a messianic sense of mission: when Chaves gave out the various instructions, he further realized that those who did it for money were the ones who did the real work, while the others were there as window-dressing: two of the professionals left the bar a few seconds before the rest and by the time they had walked a hundred yards were some good distance ahead: when the larger group, each member allotted a specific task, got to the corner of Calle Paso, the first two had disappeared from view: four of the amateurs posted themselves, in twos, on the street corners: the last remaining professional went to the corner with Calle Corrientes, which was where the police were likely to appear from if anyone called them, facing the other two youths on the opposite pavement: if Triste was dependent on anyone from that moment on, it was on that youth, who had said his name was Héctor, and his keenness of hearing: he carried out his instructions without flinching when the agreed moment came: half past five on the dot: the tar bomb, the attempt by some passersby to grab him and immobilize him, the ensuing struggle and simultaneous confirmation that the first step had been successful, and, with a violent contortion, the lurch free to throw the second object, the one intended to make a big bang and throw up lots of smoke, the explosive that was going to make everyone run, letting him escape and at the same time letting Chaves' two principal operators carry out the task assigned them: Triste threw the bomb, heard it explode, heard people screaming, and paused before turning tail to snatch a glance at the watchmaker's shop: what he saw did not get the better of his instinct for survival and he did not think twice about taking to his heels, but his heart was pounding: the spectacle that for a split second had riveted him to the ground bore no resemblance to what he had imagined: he had thrown a genuine, deadly bomb, and had almost certainly just killed a man: in the shop window, the glass shattered into a thousand glinting splinters, was the figure of a man hurled backwards by a devastating blast, his spine broken and left hanging on his chair as if folded in two, his head lolling between his shoulder blades and his outstretched arms dangling on either side, pointing towards the ground: everything was spattered with blood: the red of the carnage still before his eyes, Cristóbal suddenly found himself, not knowing how, at Once railway station: no one was following him, at least not as far as he could tell: he went to a ticket-office window and bought a return ticket to Castelar: when he got there he would change platforms and come back: more than an hour would have elapsed, which would give him time to think, and things would have quietened down: all the same, on the return journey he got out a couple of stations before the terminus from which he had originally set off, just in case, and walked two hundred yards before hailing a taxi to take him to Simón's café

if he'd been sent to kill a man without being told, how much more risky and undercover, Triste reflected, must the parallel operation have been: next day's papers, plus a detailed analysis of the information given, allowed him to piece together what had really happened: two men had been killed, not one: the first was his victim: the watchmaker, a man of peaceful habits, with no known political connections, had died just to distract people's attention: the murder victim who mattered was his neighbour on the third floor, Jewish like him but in addition a leader of the Communist Party and a well-known intellectual: two men - now Triste understood why the professionals had gone on ahead as they left the bar - had gone up to the victim's apartment: Triste worked out how their movements fitted in with his: at the moment he had thrown the tar bomb they, hearing the commotion in the street, had rung the door bell: the man had come to the door and, after asking who was there, had pushed to one side the metal disk covering the peephole and had put his left eye to it: on the other side was the barrel of a gun: apart from using a silencer, the shot had coincided with the bomb that had cut short the watchmaker's life: the bullet entered the upper half of the eye cavity and went right through his skull, hitting the wall behind the victim's back: the men had not left by the stairs but had gone up on to the roof terrace, from where they climbed on to the terrace of an adjoining building, making their exit into Calle Corrientes

Chaves did not put in an appearance for some time after: with clockwork precision, on the first day of the following month Triste was woken by his neighbour Fernando, who informed him a man was waiting to see him in the front room: he had been sent by the priest, by St. Augustine, just to deliver an envelope: the thirty thousand pesos that were his due: not a note of apology or explanation: full of vague forebodings, Triste decided to open a savings account that same day: and so he did, spending the next few mornings taking his money into the bank in instalments, so as not to arouse suspicion: despite his varied and harsh experience of life, he had not cottoned on to the fact that the banknotes bore no stamp or smell or other indication of their provenance, and that no one was going to ask questions about a sum which, though quite out of the ordinary for him, was a perfectly normal amount to have in an account: he came to this sudden realization after making four or five small deposits, whereupon he took in the whole of the rest of his savings, three hundred thousand pesos, and paid it into his account all at once: the bank clerk smiled at him, counted the money, made a note in Triste's passbook, another note in a big ledger, stamped them both and handed Cristóbal back his book with a "thank you sir: good morning," before going back to sorting the papers in front of him

Chaves reappeared in the café in Calle Salta one rainy night almost at the end of the month, nodded to everyone, ordered a whisky, drank it, paid and went out: Triste went after him, and found him waiting for him in a nearby doorway; "there's another bar on the corner," Triste indicated, walking straight past: the man in the trenchcoat followed him: when they were sitting facing each other over a table, each with a glass in front of them, Cristóbal asked what he had been dying to ask for so long: "Chaves, why didn't you tell me I was meant to kill him?": "if I'd told you, would you have done it?": "I don't know; but I had the right to know, didn't I?": "Triste, you had the right to nothing, and you have the right to nothing now; I bought you, remember? still getting your cash every month? right? so you're still bought, you've still got no rights, I'm the one who's got the rights round here": "you bought me, Chaves? and how much did you pay? thirty thousand a month? that's just a rental: how many months' pay have I had? you can have the lot back and that's the end of it, we'll each go our separate ways, OK?": "hang on a minute, my dear young Triste: you can't do that: that would have been OK before: now you've got a murder on your hands and I'm in the know: you can't back out and quit this business as if it were any old job, not now": "so you've put the screws on me, have you, Padre?": "what did I hear you say, Cristóbal?": "Padre; I said Padre: because you're a priest, aren't you?": "and how do you know that?": "I go to church a lot and I saw you once": "you'd better forget what

73

you saw, Triste: I've got a lot of influence, a lot of clout: and anyway I've got something to accuse you of to the police: murder: and what can you accuse me of to the police? of being a priest? that's a perfectly legal occupation as far as I know: they'd take you for crazy: are you going to go to the police and say - he's a priest? really, they'll say, and what does that make you? an anarchist? an anticlerical agitator? that information will get you nowhere, Triste: I'm a priest, you're a killer of poor, defenceless old Jews, got it?": "yes": "good: now you can take a little holiday: I'll be in touch: look after yourself, Triste": and he got up and left: so much would happen before they met again

Chapter 9. Token of Love

What does the flow of time matter if
there was one peak, one thrill, one evening?
J.L. BORGES, *Page in Remembrance of*
Colonel Suárez

she was called, or went by the name of, Malena, a name full
of nostalgic associations for anyone who has ever taken an
interest in the curious poetic underworld of the tango: "no
one sings tangos like Malena,/ in every line she leaves her
heart," went the song written long before the night Triste
met her at one of the local dance halls where he
systematically spent every Saturday night, dance halls like
the Carlos Gardel Sports and Social Club in Ituzaingó,
where the sports promised by the title were restricted to
cards and dice: such clubs, or establishments like the Tango
Bar in Lanús, next to the station, functioned principally as
places where single people could meet someone of the
opposite sex, in addition to the staging of dance competi-
tions which threw up many a star performer of that popular
art, most of them simply concerned with finding an outlet
for an exhibitionism that compensated or sublimated the
unsatisfied seductive urges haunting and hounding those
machos who were so macho they could only talk to other
machos, and who usually ended up going home to bed alone,
more often than not in houses or hostels or tenement rooms
shared with their ageing mothers: Triste, who felt capable of
taking on almost anything and by that stage had a murder to
his credit - a murder which, if it made him sleep uneasily at
night, did so because of the possibility of Chaves grassing on
him, not because it had made a deep impression on his
conscience, toughened by the countless humiliations he had

suffered since birth - nevertheless was genuinely terrified of women: whenever he plucked up courage to invite some stranger - for they were almost all strangers - to dance, he would be so overwhelmed by fear of doing or saying the wrong thing, that he would execute all the steps indicated by the music with a spellbinding precision and, when the music stopped, would return the lady in question to the well of silence from which he had dragged her a few minutes before, himself returning to the restless, dreary reveries of the lonely

Malena - it had to be someone - finally rescued him from his vicious circle: she was the first woman who, after almost five years of identical Saturday nights, ignoring the decorum required of a young lady speaking to a gentleman she had never met before, whose name she did not know, with whom she had only exchanged a brief "may I have the pleasure...?", "certainly", cutting through the threadbare formulae of a superfluous politeness, had been brazen enough to say to him while they were dancing: "why don't you let go a bit? you're a great dancer, you know: but you'd be even better if you'd let the music carry you: that's what it's for": as if in a mirror, Triste saw the blood come rushing to his face, followed by an uncontrollable cold sweat: "look into my eyes and forget you're dancing, will you?": "yes, I will," he plucked up courage to say, looking into the girl's eyes without telling her it was the first time he'd looked into a girl's eyes: when the dance was over, she smiled and said, "aren't you going to offer me a drink?": "of course," said Triste, floundering in indecision, "of course: what would you like?": she ordered a *Cuba libre*: "and a big gin on the rocks for me," he indicated, before venturing the seemingly unfathomable question: "how old are you?", asking her name, telling himself he thought she was beautiful and her age didn't matter because in any case she was incredibly young: "my name's Malena and I'm over eighteen: what about you?": "my name's Cristóbal; I'm over eighteen too:

well eighteen anyway, though I look older": "and I'm twenty, though I look younger": he felt embarrassed to tell her his nickname but then thought if she's going to be my girlfriend and we're going to go out together, I'd better not keep it from her; someone else is bound to come out with it and that'll be worse: "know something? people call me Triste: I don't know why": "because you look sad, Triste, or because you are sad": they spent a while talking about nothing in particular, about any old thing, till he remembered and reminded her that it was still early and they could take a taxi and go and have a meal downtown, and then go on to dance somewhere more posh than where they were now: she realized, without totting up the exact figures, that meant an expensive evening out: "you've got money," she stated, looking at the boy: "yes": "have you got a job?": "no, I haven't got a job: I earn my living; I mean I haven't got a job like most people's, if you see what I mean": "sort of: not a pimp, are you?": "no, how could I be a pimp?": he asked the question in good faith, thinking she must be able to see that someone as shy as he would be useless as a pimp: though, he would reflect later, she must have seen something in him to ask the question: even at the end, he never came to see that she was only projecting onto him what she knew, what she was, used to repaying men with her body and her earnings as a whore: "are we going downtown then?": "let's go"

the night was a long one, Triste had never talked so much to anyone: he kept things like his relationship with Chaves to himself, but told her other things, from earlier in his life, till then forgotten, and there was a moment, which at first he took for a sign of incredible weakness and later came to appreciate for what it was, a moment of unusual sincerity and rare strength of mind, which was responsible for almost all the tokens of happiness he would receive later on, when he managed to tell her squarely and unfalteringly that he had never slept with a woman: when it was almost dawn they found a hotel where you could rent rooms by the hour: he ordered a bottle of gin and some glasses to be brought up to the room: he was smoking and drinking, without even having taken his jacket off, reflecting on this new turn of events, when she came out of the bathroom completely naked except for her high-heeled shoes and stood in front of him, as he slowly looked up, caressing her gently with his eyes from her perfectly formed ankles to the quizzical look he wasn't expecting to find: "do you want me?" the girl asked, needing reassurance: Triste, without moving from the sofa, without making any gesture to her, without proffering a single word, let trickle down his cheeks the tears he had held back for years, for an eternity, the tears he had held back at Rosario Artola's death, in their stead stolidly reciting the prayers that were part of her legacy, the tears he had held back as he went through the pockets of Don Lauro lying dead on the ground in a corner of the Plaza de Mayo, the tears he had held back so as to see clearly the face of the man Marcos Peña had sent to crush his hands: "really? you want me that much?" Malena insisted: he replied with a nod of the head, still weeping, and held out his hands to take hers: and then the tears started to roll down her cheeks too, long, hot tears, as she held Triste's hands, kneeling in front of him, their two mouths, their four eyes very close, joined by that baptism of tears, the one sacrament that would unite them for ever

he took her to live with him: she had practically nothing, just a suitcase with some clothes in it at a boarding-house: they went to pick it up and brought it back to the tenement: he wanted to rent an apartment in Buenos Aires proper - by that time such a thing was within his means - but it would have to wait till later: right now he needed to stay where he was, where he could easily be found: they celebrated their decision throughout the course of the second night, in Simón Castro's café: then they began their honeymoon in a nearby hotel, where they spent most of the time talking and making love: telling each other their painful, difficult stories

she didn't tell him everything then: she waited for past acts, the gestures and wounds of forgotten days, to work their way to the tip of her tongue so they could be communicated to Triste: and Malena - whose real name, according to the papers he had gone through when she wasn't looking, was Clotilde Bárcena - told the story of her adolescence spent with a man who fulfilled the multiple functions of father, husband, lover and pimp, a man to whom she had thought herself fatally joined for life but whom, when it came to it, she had left without fear or guilt: without either of the emotions he had tried to instil in her to stop her leaving him, though - so Malena assured him - the separation had effectively occurred long before it had materialized in her mind as a conscious decision: "but," Cristóbal wanted to ascertain, "he made you walk the streets, whore for him, and you did?": "I would have done anything for him, like I would for you now," the girl's reply was not a self-justification or request for forgiveness, but a statement of fact, a declaration of the spirited, unconditional nature of her love: "and who was that man, Malena? never mind, if you don't want to tell me, you don't need to": in his anguish, Triste wanted to know all the details: "I don't mind telling you: his name was - or is, it's ages since I last had news of him - Fidel Sánchez, and he took me to live with him in Berisso when I was twelve and didn't have a roof over my head or anyone to turn to, after leaving my mother's because there were too many of us in the shack: too many mouths to feed and too many bodies for beds, you see: and I went with him because I liked him: no one had ever cared for me before and he cared for me, he looked after me: he gave me what he could, which wasn't much, it's true, but I gave him the same, what I could, which wasn't much either": a thick, haunting silence, and Malena went on, bringing the story to an end, rounding it off with a moral: "and anyway, Triste, it's such a wonderful thing to be able to make someone else feel good, make life easier for them; I'd get home and he'd be looking at me lovingly, so lovingly, till he stopped being so loving, went cold - maybe it was guilt that made him go cold, or fear of getting put inside - and I changed too, you see, like I was his mirror-image: I went cold too and one day I left and that was the last I heard of him"

the day came when Malena came back late, very late one night: Triste was sitting up waiting for her, at the table, drinking gin and asking himself how all this would end, his living with a woman, his apparently eternal holidays: she came in the door and smiled at him: "here," she said, holding out a small parcel, "it's for you; and so is this," a five-hundred-peso note, folded in half: Triste opened the parcel and looked at the cuff links inside, looked at the note, looked up at her and said "thanks": and she: "I wanted to give you a present: I've never given you a present, and that's the only way I know how to make money, by whoring": Triste got up, went over to her and put his arms round her: with his head on Malena's shoulder, facing the other way so she wouldn't see his moist eyes, he repeated "thanks": there would be other days like that, sorties born of Malena's desire to do for Triste what no one had ever done for him before, not of necessity or desperation or financial need: every now and then she would come home late with a present, and they would make love: he, as if needing to ratify his possession of a body he felt escaping him: she, as if needing to ratify the integrity of a body which, although hers, she regarded as not entirely her own property: if someone had asked her at the time, Malena would doubtless have insisted that her whoring was a token of love: that was how Triste interpreted it too, and it was in that belief that he would always accept her material offerings with moist eyes finally the day came when Malena did not come back: the anxiety of the first few hours of waiting gave way to concern, surprise, incredulity, the desperate attempt to work out what he might have done to upset her, hurling every possible accusation, insult and reproach at her, missing her, crying (perhaps not so much on account of her, on account of her absence, as on account of the long, lonely days that would inevitably follow), the first clouds in his memory of their life together

it was Fernando, his elderly neighbour, who over the years had become such a good friend, who brought him the newspaper on the third day: in all that time Triste had not moved out of the room, filling the wait he knew was utterly futile with drinks of gin and long periods of semi-consciousness, no matter what the time of day: the paper had a photo of Malena taken some time before, together with a report on the violent end met by Clotilde Bárcena: her lifeless body had been found in the outlying town of Ensenada, stabbed, inside a car which had earlier been reported stolen by its owner: practically nothing was known about the victim except her name: the coroner calculated that the murder must have taken place between six and nine o'clock on the morning of the day after Malena had left the tenement never to return: Fernando came in with the paper folded so the photo was the first thing visible: "it's her, isn't it, Triste?": "yes, Fernando, that's Malena," Triste heard himself say, distancing himself from events so as to be able to take them in, one bit at a time: "she's been murdered, Fernando: stabbed": "I know, Cristóbal, I've just read it; I'm sorry about it, but someone had to tell you, didn't they?": "of course; thanks, my friend": in Ensenada, Triste thought: too close to Berisso - they were neighbouring towns - for it to be coincidence: he sent Fernando away, washed under the spurt of ice-cold water that served as a shower, got dressed, went to the station and had a coffee and gin in the bar inside before buying his ticket: he wasn't going to Buenos Aires: he was going to Berisso

Triste knew how to get information when he wanted it: it took him just an hour to find a barman who knew Fidel Sánchez: "why do you want to know about Sánchez, man? you don't look like a cop," the man said to him: "I'm not interested in Sánchez but in the woman he used to live with: and you're right, I'm not a cop: this is personal": "revenge?": "something like that": "she's been murdered, you know," a client following the conversation chimed in, "it's in today's paper, with a photo and everything; though she was prettier than that": "you knew them too?": "sure: I've lived round these parts for seventy years: do you think there's anyone I don't know?": "no, right...": "so now you know she's dead and you won't be able to find her, if that's what you were after," the old man concluded: "I wanted to see the man, Fidel Sánchez, too": neither the bar-tender nor the obliging old man burst out laughing: they exchanged looks and simply smiled knowingly: it was the younger man who finally spoke: "look: I don't know what you've come for, but what I do know is that you're not going to find either of them: Fidel Sánchez's been dead for a year": a big gulp of gin and Triste's inevitable question: "and how did he die?": "stabbed: seventeen times: by his woman, before she took off and vanished into the blue till yesterday: the police were after her, and they finally tracked her down in a car, full of stab wounds: the same as she gave Fidel Sánchez: anything else you want to know?": "no thanks, I don't want to know anything else, I'd rather not have found out what you've just told me, but it's too late now and anyway it's best to know, don't you think?": "who knows?"

at that point a third man, so far unobserved in the shadows at the back of the bar, drinking wine in a huge glass, his face half-buried in the pages of a sports magazine, came up to Triste and asked him: "did you know the woman?": "yes": "know her well, I mean?": "we lived together for the last few months, but I don't think I knew her all that well": right from the very first question Triste knew the man was a cop; he wasn't taken aback, and had no thoughts of resisting, when he heard him say "would you kindly accompany me to the police station?": "of course," he replied

Chapter 10. Family Reunion

Patio that exists no more. The wet
Evening brings me the voice, the voice I regret,
Of my father who returns and is not dead.
J.L. BORGES, *The Rain*

the courteous distance of "kindly accompany me to the
police station" vanished the minute they left the dingy bar
and went out into the street, giving way to that authoritarian
but at the same time whining tone of voice that characterizes
the police the world over: "it's some way to the station," the
man said, possibly trying to mark time while he worked out
what to do with Cristóbal (of whose innocence or stupidity
he was wholly convinced), possibly prodding him in the hope
of a bribe: Triste's reply took him aback: "aren't there any
taxis in this dump?": "this isn't a dump," he replied, his local
pride wounded: "and of course there are taxis, here's one":
Triste didn't think twice: with an imperious flourish of his
right hand, he hailed the cab and opened the back door:
"you first," he said to his captor: "that's the limit!" snapped
the right arm of the law, asking, "do you think I'm so thick
I'd get in and leave you standing out there on the
pavement?": "have it your way": Triste was worn out, worn
out by the days of waiting and drinking and trying to forget;
worn out too by what he had just learnt about Malena and
Fidel Sánchez, worn out and flattened by all the dirt she had
concealed from him, perhaps not out of malice but in any
case unnecessarily; too worn out to put up a fight, to
challenge the cop's insulting tone of voice by insulting him
back: "tell the driver where we're going and don't worry
about the fare, I'll pay": "take us to the police station," the
man ordered, vowing he'd have it in for this smartass
prisoner: there's no way you're getting out of a month's time

in Devoto Jail, that's for sure, he brooded

when they got to the gloomy building, he handed Triste over to the officer on duty, instructing him: "I'm off to see the Inspector: get his details, forty-eight hours for the time being while we check his file": they took down his particulars, surname, forename, address, age, kept his identity card and took prints of all ten fingers: the pale, morose individual responsible for this last step handed him, to get the ink off his fingers, a piece of towelling which must have been used for the same purpose by several hundred people before him: the net effect was to spread the ink more evenly over his hands: it was then that he understood something old Lauro had once tried to explain, without the boy really knowing what he meant: "that's what the clink's for, to make you feel dirty": he would learn more about such things in the days to come: how in prison the struggle to keep clean physically is vital: feeling dirty is the first subtle step towards feeling defeated, and you have to train all five senses to detect it: the smell of prison, which clings to your clothes and skin long after getting out, is the most crushing of the system's inevitable triumphs: it seeps into you without your realizing: you get your first shock when, after taking a normal bath or shower in a hotel or back at home, you sniff the undershirt you've taken off a few minutes before: it smells of prison, a smell compounded of urine from irreparably stained mattresses, stale sweat, mildewy leather from permanently damp feet, the occasional uncontrollable discharge of semen, voluntary or otherwise, all permeated by the omnipresent stench of bleach, slopped day in day out over the same loathsome concrete tiles, to the point where it can no longer eliminate but only add to the grime

after the routine identification procedures, they led him off to a big communal cell, at that time housing two other inmates: a drunk - sleeping it off obscenely splay-legged on the solid concrete ledge, some twenty inches high and perhaps two to two-and-a-half feet wide, built into, or out of, the concrete floor and wall, a ledge which served as bed, seat, table and any other item of furniture that might be replaced by its immovable hulk - and an evil-looking man with whom Cristóbal exchanged not a single word in the course of the long hours they spent together and whose stare made him do his best not to doze off: one of the side walls between the door and the wretched bunk did not end at a right angle to the floor but in a gutter moulded in the same almost stone-like substance of which the whole room was built, into which all the inmates' bodily excretions had to be deposited, solid or liquid, with a total lack of modesty should one's fellows not, in a tactful gesture of solidarity, avert their gaze and pretend to concentrate on some unknown con-undrum: nothing else happened for two days, during which the guards handed them, as the state's sole contribution to the upkeep of those in its care, two mugs of weak coffee and two stale loaves of bread: they were offered the possibility of buying additional food in a nearby café, at outrageous prices, if they had the cash: Triste could have done so, but preferred not to give the other prisoners the idea he was well off

eventually, the judge arrived who was dealing with the preliminary investigations into Clotilde Bárcena's murder: after nearly three hours of making statements, giving his cross-examiner all the information he had about the victim, he was allowed to make a phone call: he rang Simón Castro, briefly put him in the picture and asked him, casually and as if the idea had just occurred to him, to let Chaves know, because maybe he had the influence to get him off the hook: Simón agreed with his reasoning, which coincided with his own suspicions about Chaves' activities ("you were quite right to tell me," Chaves flaunted his influence pompously; "I'll do what I can for the boy, and I can assure you that's quite a bit": he did absolutely nothing, but on the first day of the month Triste's wages, as he would later discover, were punctually paid into his account, which he had told no one about and whose number he had kept a jealously guarded secret): Cristóbal's statements merely confirmed the notion that he was as innocent as a newborn babe but, in the absence of better leads, it was a good idea to keep him on the books: the thirty days he spent in Villa Devoto Jail, in the incredible building in Calle Bermúdez which at the time housed detainees awaiting trail, were on account of an unfounded charge of insulting behaviour and attempted bribery of an officer of the law which, there being no witnesses other than the protagonists, was at the same time irrefutable: a different judge dealt with this new case against Triste, a judge visibly embarrassed by the vicissitudes of his trade, which obliged him to give credence to the police rather than the individual citizen, over a story which - as he knew full well - had never happened: the same judge pronounced a sentence of thirty days when he had already been in prison for twenty-two, and Triste was let out after serving eight days of his sentence, which was exceptionally light on account of the accused's lack of a criminal record: but during those thirty days spent in jail, Triste had an encounter

he saw him, without knowing why his sight had struck him enough to make him turn round and go on staring, the minute he got out of the police van that had transported him from the cell in Berisso to the prison in the capital: Triste did not give the man's face another thought as he was marched off by a prison officer through the thousand and one offices which, being the bureaucratic antechamber to a prolonged void, did not alarm him or make him feel any need to speed things up: in the first office, he went through an identification procedure similar to the one he had gone through at the police station: when he had finished implanting his fingerprints on the appropriate form, he was handed a cloth which, had the idea not been totally absurd, he could have sworn was the same one he had used in Berisso for the same impossible hygienic purposes: in another office he handed over those personal belongings deemed to be dangerous - knife, belt (the latter a high-priority object on account of its use by prisoners to hang themselves or string up other prisoners), shoelaces, tie, key - or not needed while in prison - identity card, scraps of paper with phone numbers scribbled on them, three thousand two hundred pesos in a wallet with Rosario and Malena's photos, which he minded parting with more than he would ever have imagined: finally they handed him his prison equipment - spoon, aluminium plate, thin blanket - and led him off to what was to be his destination: Cell Block 2: it was designed without individual cells, but with several beds to a room like a hospital ward though with no curtains or screens to provide the necessary privacy, plus a storage area for the consumables the men had to share: food parcels sent by relatives, bars of chocolate, utensils for making coffee or *maté*: when they unlocked the door to let him in, Triste said in a loud, clear voice to all the men staring at him, and some who remained sunk in thought or absorbed in a newspaper or cheap novel, "good evening, gentlemen": they said "good evening" back, in unison, and he gave them all a smile before adding, "my name is Cristóbal Artola, they call me Triste, I'm going to spend some time with you," and stepping inside

his encounter with the man whose identity he had half-intuited on his arrival took place on the second day, in the exercise yard: Triste had latched on to an experienced, good-natured prisoner who had spent some considerable time there without having yet come up for trial, thanks to the proverbial slow course of Argentine justice and the inefficiency of the defence lawyer he had been provided with on legal aid (one much in need of legal aid himself) and

whom he had had to accept, having run out of money to go
on hiring a private lawyer: the prisoner, Agustín Botazzo,
seemed to know almost everybody inside, with few excep-
tions, and had struck up conversation with Triste right at the
start, when the men were introducing themselves and
explaining their cases to the new arrival: "and what brought
you here?": "a trumped-up charge," Cristóbal was taken
aback to find his reply met with grins and snickers on all
sides: "what's the matter? what's so funny?": "don't worry,"
said the one who would soon become his friend, "we're only
laughing because what you've just said is what we all say; and
it's true, of course: we're all in here on some trumped-up
charge or other": "all of you?": "all of us": "and what have
you all been charged with?": "that's irrelevant: it might be
relevant if the charge were true, but since it's not ... and it
might be relevant if you wanted to find out about the man
who filed the charge: the charge would tell you something
about him all right; but not about us": "you're right, of
course," Triste admitted: "sure I'm right, but that doesn't
change anything: we're still here"

it was the start of a long conversation without beginning or
end, which ended only to start all over again: Botazzo was in
Villa Devoto on a false charge of murder, but that was
immaterial: when Triste went out into the daylight on the
morning of the second day and saw the man, he thought of
asking his new mate who he was, sure he would know, but he
ended up staring at the man whose sight so disturbed him
without saying a word: in a corner of the yard where
throughout the year men shaved in the open air, in their
undershirts, there was a piece of mirror-glass, not fastened
to the wall with screws or brackets, which would have turned
it into a magnificent weapon, but pressed into the concrete
when still wet and now part of its surface: it was to that
mirror that Triste went after half an hour of intense, fixed
staring, just to remind himself what he looked like, to check

that, given the delicate nature of the matter, his memory was not playing tricks: the face he saw was the same as the face he remembered, though had it been in his power to choose he would have preferred, now as always, to be someone else

having checked the idiosyncrasies of his physical features, he turned round, anxiously seeking the man out: when he caught sight of him, he was at the far end of the yard: he had for some time been resolutely and steadily pacing up and down: the self-imposed exercise of a man unable to adapt to the sedentary nature of prison life and needing to invent activities to keep himself, if not exactly fit, in reasonable shape till the time his release should come, as it surely would: Triste walked straight across the yard to intercept the man's path, which he did almost in the middle of the spacious rectangle: "good morning," he said, forcing the other man to look up: "good morning," the latter replied, as he looked at the boy and went on looking, unable to take his eyes off the face before him, just as Triste had been unable to take his eyes off his face from the start: he looked, remembered what he himself looked like, recoiled, tried to avert the discovery that had already been made: it was Cristóbal who spoke: "you're Manuel Lema, aren't you?" holding out his hand and accepting his father's dumbfounded nod as an acceptable reply in the circumstances: after coughing loudly and clearing his throat for several minutes - the lengthy journey required for a word to reach the air that makes it a word - he managed to give shape to the monosyllable "yes": "I'm Cristóbal Artola and I'm your son: do you realize that?": "of course I do: I've got eyes too: just like yours: how's Rosario? because you're her son and mine, aren't you?": "yes: my mother died seven, eight years ago ... I don't know exactly, in '54: before she died she called out to you, shouted your name: she was conscious for just a second, and that's what she chose to do with it": Lema looked at the ground, motionless, listening: "it's true she loved me and I didn't love her, but if I'd known she was pregnant ...": "supposing you had known ... would you have stayed?": a heavy silence: "no, I wouldn't have stayed in that case either": "so in the end things were better as they were: you're not my father": "no, kid, I'm not your father: I'm not in a position to be anyone's father, OK?": "I'm sorry: I always wanted to meet you; and it's true what everyone always said: we look just like each other, don't we?": "yes, but that makes no difference; I'm not your father": "OK": Triste turned his back on Manuel Lema and spent the rest of his time in the exercise yard staring blankly up at the sky: when he got back to the cell block, he flung himself on his bed and cried: he cried silently all day, till he fell asleep exhausted

that same night, Manuel Lema was murdered in his bed by a fellow prisoner who stabbed him beneath the left nipple with the sharpened handle of a spoon: clearly someone who knew what he was doing: the heart had been perforated

Chapter 11. Disappeared

so hard it rained blood/
blood rained all over my country
from the veins severed by the assassins/
from the hearts that still remember/
JUAN GELMAN, *Note IX*

Triste's return to the world of the supposedly free, of those
with and without illusions, of those respected for being
winners and those despised for being losers, Triste's return
to the tenement, to the empty room, to the cafés in the city
centre and particularly the café in Calle Salta, was met with
no more fuss and ceremony than the bear hug and slaps on
the back he received from Simón Castro, convinced his
friend's short stay inside was due, not to his innocence,
which had never been doubted, but to the good offices of the
august Chaves: Cristóbal neither confirmed nor refuted the
idea, having his own doubts but feeling unable to deny what
the other affirmed, for lack of evidence either way: besides,
his relationship of dependence with regard to the man who
was his boss, the fact that the money had kept on coming in
while he was out of the picture, made him reluctant to
believe what his instincts told him was true: the subject was
never properly discussed: anyway the only person who knew
the truth was Chaves, the only person who had lied from the
start: they never really discussed Malena's puzzling fate
either, and Triste chose to say nothing about his encounter,
his brief crossing of paths with Manuel Lema, hours before
the latter's descent into final darkness, as if rounding off the
life story of Rosario Artola, now definitively dead and
buried: Simón Castro had avoided any mention of that side
of Triste's existence since the day when, out of mere
curiosity, he had asked where his parents came from, a
common question in a city with a largely immigrant

population: "I didn't have parents; just a mother, and she never talked about her past," Cristóbal had answered, speaking from experience at the same time as anticipating a confirmation still to come

Chaves appeared in Castro's bar a week after Triste's release: he gave everyone a casual nod and made no reference to the events of the last six weeks: when no one was listening, in the course of the heated argument about sports which engrossed all the customers present for two whole hours, he indicated that he needed to see Triste, slipping him the now routine message: "we've got to talk: tomorrow, at four, in the Tortoni": "fine," Cristóbal complied

the press of the time helps reconstruct the sequence of events whose course was decided by that meeting: Triste and Chaves met at the said café in Avenida de Mayo on the 22nd August 1962 - exactly ten years before the massacre at Trelew, in a kind of ominous anniversary of the future - and Felipe Vallese was last seen alive seven days later, on the 29th: "we've got a big job coming up," Chaves made clear straightaway, "you're going to have to earn all those months of wages in one fell swoop": Triste took a few minutes to digest the implications of the warning, "what's the job to be this time?" he asked before himself warning, "if somebody's got to be killed, I hope I'll be given advance notice": "not going to get difficult, are you?": "no, of course not; I'll do whatever's got to be done: I'd just like to know what it is a bit beforehand; that's fair enough, isn't it? preparing oneself spiritually, I think it's called: if it's a right of the man about to die, it ought to be a right of the man who's going to see to it": "so you want rights and all?" Chaves beamed patronizingly before launching into the slogan of the day: "we're here to promulgate the rights of the whole nation, Triste: that's what you're paid for, OK?": "sure, sure... just get down to business, Chaves, don't let's get into some footling argument": "all right, my boy, I can tell you it's a kidnapping: a trade union leader, a commie": "a commie? sure? sure he's not a Peronist? sure he's a commie, Chaves?": "you can take my word for it": "you can stuff your word up your arse; go on: out with the whole story then": "he's a youngster, about your age, but a real troublemaker: the son of Italian immigrants, a metalworker, who doesn't take things lying down: you'll have a hard time getting him into the car without attracting too much attention, though it's a quiet district, not much traffic, and the job's to be done at night": "and then what?": "that's it, we hand him over to the appropriate authorities: he's not to be killed: they want him alive"

at eleven o'clock on the night of the 29th August, Felipe Vallese left home with his brother Italo, talking about politics on the way: they walked down Calle Morelos till the crossing with Canalejas: there they parted company: Italo was going on to Plaza Irlanda, Felipe continued on his normal route down Canalejas to get to the factory where he worked and where he was due to start the night shift: just after the intersection with Calle Trelles, and about fifty yards before Donato Alvárez, Chaves' gang sprang out on him: while the priest stayed at the wheel, waiting with the engine running, Triste and Héctor, the same Héctor who had acted as look-out in the pogrom against the old watchmaker, wrestled with their victim for a few minutes: Vallese clung on to a tree with all his might while his assailants beat him mercilessly to wear down his resistance: two of the trade unionist's acquaintances, who caught sight of what was going on from the café on the corner of Canalejas and Donato Alvárez and thought it was a mugging, ran out to come to the young man's assistance as he struggled valiantly: Triste, seeing them appear, pointed a pistol in their direction and let out a "beat it, you two; just keep out of this" that left little room for doubt: intimidated, the two men retreated, as the so-called Héctor savagely pounded the back of the worker's neck with the butt of his gun, and the latter's arms went limp as he slumped to the ground, unconscious: between them, covering their rear, they grasped the unconscious youth by the armpits, one on either side, and lugged him to the car, which had drawn up alongside: calmly, now that all was clear, they bundled him into the back of the car, pushing him down between the back seat and the seat in front, on the floor: Triste got in next to Chaves, while his fellow assailant got in behind, his feet resting on Vallese's inert body: they drove off at top speed in the direction of San Martín, where they were to hand over their charge to the sadly celebrated Mobile Brigades: so they did: Felipe Vallese was never seen again

after they had transferred the hostage to a car without number plates, occupied by the men from the San Martín Brigades, Chaves made for the centre to drop Héctor, or whatever his name was, off near San Juan and Boedo, carrying on to leave Triste near Simón Castro's café, which was where he assumed he wanted to go: "what about you, Triste? OK if I drop you off near the café?": "fine, I could do with a drink before I go home": on the way, Chaves broke the silence just once to observe casually: "that little lamb we've just picked up had been to Russia and all": the remark was gratuitous, but he knew Cristóbal would feel better and would do a better job if he were given certain assurances: even if these took the form of statements that were quite unverifiable, his fear of betraying his mother's memory made him latch on to them, investing them with a justificatory value they did not have: the priest had sussed out this blind spot in Cristóbal, and had no compunction about exploiting the discovery to clinch the explanations his collaborator (as he preferred to call those who offered him their services without questioning the ethics or consequences of their acts) occasionally demanded before committing himself further: before that night was over, Chaves had the opportunity of discovering another weak spot in Triste: they were speeding down Hipólito Yrigoyen when he came out with the question: "and what happened with the girl in the end, Triste? with Malena, I mean: she turned out to have a bit of a past, I gather": "leave Malena out of it, Chaves, she's dead: don't cast stones: don't sling mud at those that are cleaner than you: you've got a bit of a past behind you too, remember: so lay off criticizing her, she was worth more than either of us: if she killed the guy, she must have had her reasons: I loved her and I've got nothing to reproach her for, OK?": "OK, Cristóbal, and don't get wound up: I didn't mean to offend": "everything you do, you do without meaning to, Chaves; and one of these days someone's going to get you for one of those little blunders": they didn't speak to each other till, as they passed Entre Ríos, Cristóbal said, "stop on the corner," and got out

Cristóbal hadn't expected the press to give so much space to Vallese's kidnap: he found it hard to understand how a man he had overpowered in a matter of minutes and whom no one had made much of an effort to defend, even though he was armed, could be so important: all that about him having been to Russia must be true, but the papers said nothing about it (still, everyone knew the press was a pack of lies): what they did say was that the worker was a Peronist, and they referred to him as "disappeared", perhaps the first usage of the term in the two-edged sense it was to acquire with subsequent wider use: in effect, Vallese showed no signs of life - and never would from that moment on - but there were no signs of his being dead either - nor would there ever be - and for a dead man to be dead, he had to have a body, had to have left behind him an empty, lifeless, useless body: no body of Vallese was found, no Vallese was found, all that existed was his disappearance, his absence, confused statements about the kidnapping, references to the San Martín Brigades, denunciations of torture inflicted on various members of the victim's family: people he had never set eyes on: he realized the others, Vallese's brother, his wife, had been taken away by colleagues of his or by members of the police not averse to the use of torture, not averse to clubbing people, breaking their bones, mutilating them, reducing them to a pulp in order to make them talk - Triste didn't know too much about torture, his imaginings fell short of the reality: he would find out for himself at a later stage of his career, almost at the end: the action he had taken part in was, as on the previous occasion, just part of a larger operation: he also realized the man he had beaten up and bundled into the car would never be seen again by those demanding his release, his friends, relatives, lawyers: that was part and parcel of the dirty profession to which he had contracted his services and which paid such high dividends, so he pushed the matter out of his mind and busied himself with more pleasurable matters, like the state of his bank account or his definitive move to Buenos Aires: if the idea of leaving the tenement for a place downtown had seemed a more than reasonable proposition when he was with Malena, it seemed much less rosy and even senseless now she was dead: in the tenement he had old Fernando, and Doña Amanda who had been so close to his mother when she was alive: near at hand he had Don Matías, the doctor or quack or whatever he was, who like Fernando had not thought twice about giving him a helping hand in moments of need: the municipal depot held the memory of Lauro, a father if ever he had had one: Malena could have filled his life in some other place, but now she was gone his friends were all-important to him: he could no more imagine living somewhere else than he could imagine not going to Simón Castro's café: he gave up the idea

he would often reproach himself for his naivety in having

ever made that initial pact with the man who now had him in his grip: it was true that he received sums of money he could never have earned so easily in any other form of employment: but it was also true that his firm intentions of never collaborating with the police had come to nought: his activities took place at a point where the distinction between politics and police ceased to exist, despite the fact that the participation of the latter was masked by patriotic rhetoric, reinforced by reference to the existence of common enemies, enemies of patriots and the police alike, enemies of the nation: he was reluctant to admit to himself that funds as handsomely endowed as those from which his salary was paid were unlikely to be dipped into so freely and regularly if they came from private sources, no matter how fanatical their owner's belief in a cause: which meant admitting that his salary was paid out the state coffers via some political branch or intelligence division not officially recognized but known to exist: the priest Chaves worked for it, probably occupying a relatively low position in the chain of command: and he, Triste, was a rank-and-file hired assassin, to whom the dirtiest jobs, the jobs no one wanted to know about, were farmed out: he was not particularly upset by that conclusion: he had never expected to command respect: the place he occupied in the world was a murky one where individual features blur and faces, clearly distinguishable by the light of day, become anonymous and unreal: an area where the notion of evil fades into non-existence and the hope of being appreciated does not arise: but he needed to go on living, and that required him to respect himself

it was round about that time he took to drinking more heavily, getting drunk and on occasions not being able to keep upright to find his way back to the tenement room: it was to drink that Simón Castro always attributed his friend's odd behaviour one night, when he decided to shut up shop early to do the rounds as a client of certain other seedy joints to which he was partial, in Triste's company: the two of them downed glass after glass of gin, laced with the odd beer to slake their thirst, but Simón was strangely lucid at three in the morning when Cristóbal stopped and stared at the wall past which they were walking: the Galician thought his buddy was about to piss against the wall when he heard him shout, " *Viva* Perón, godammit!" his eyes glued to a poster issued by the General Workers' Confederation on which, under Felipe Vallese's picture, questions were asked about his fate: " *Viva* Perón, godammit!" he shouted a second time and fell silent, as if expecting a reply: finally, with a clumsy attempt at an obscene gesture, he said, "get stuffed" to the young man on the poster, turning his back on him and saying to Simón, "let's go"

Chapter 12. The Pope

> Things are so bent
> that the poor man's life is spent
> dodging the long arm of the law.
> J. HERNANDEZ, *Martín Fierro*, Part II

Chaves, the man in the trenchcoat, was, as Cristóbal had rightly supposed, just a subaltern, a go-between, a boss only to those beneath him, to those he had to deal with and assist: a boss obliged - as shown by his firsthand involvement in the recent events whose leading lights had been Triste and the old Jewish watchmaker, Triste and Felipe Vallese - to rub his nose in the dirt alongside his recruits: there were obviously bosses, great and small, above him, men with more power, closer to the crock of gold, closer to the voice of command: the proliferation of the nameless organization of which they were part was, it seems, the decisive factor that led Chaves to introduce his subordinates to one of his superiors: "the boss wants to meet you," he told Cristóbal, "he's expecting you on Sunday, at his home out at Morón": "you make it sound as though I'm a regular house-guest": "don't worry, Triste: we'll meet in the morning at eleven, and go on together: you'll like him: he's a great man, the boss": "I'm not so sure about that, Chaves; but I'd better come if I want to keep the job, right?": "you won't regret coming"

they took the train at Once Station: on their way along Calle Mitre to the ticket office, Chaves pointed out Rivadavia's colossal mausoleum on the far side of the square: "know who's buried there, Triste?": "no, I didn't know anyone could be buried in a square": "the man buried there is Rivadavia": "a president, wasn't he?": "something like that:

the nearest you could get to it a hundred years or so ago; he was a mulatto ... coloured, a half-caste, and a lackey of the English, so they say ...": "... and who says, Chaves?": "lots of people: respectable historians, like Rosa, and people who know what they're talking about, like the boss": "look: just shut up about the boss, will you? I'm going to meet him for myself, I don't need to be told what to think": it was a short journey by train: at Morón Station, they took a bus for two, perhaps three miles: they got out in a residential suburb, where there were no more than two houses with their grounds to each block, and walked for a bit: Chaves pointed to the gateway of one such mansion, the like of which Triste had only ever seen in the movies, said, "this is it," and resolutely pressed a bell which must have rung in some distant quarter: rushing to open the gate came a man got up in the most extraordinary garb: riding boots and jodhpurs, the former black, the latter grey, and a black shirt, cut like an army shirt but with no military insignia: "come in please, the chief is expecting you," in a strong foreign accent; "you must be Señor Artola," and he held out his hand: "indeed," Triste replied, shaking the hand held out to him, "I'm Artola": then, causing Cristóbal to smile to himself: "and what about you, Father Chaves, how are you?": "fine, Kromer, thank you"

Kromer led them up the path to the house: they went inside and found themselves in a grandly furnished reception room, albeit somewhat impersonal, that looked as though it were never used: on one side was a door, smaller than the front door, leading to the rest of the building: it was to this little door that Kromer strode: he opened it and stood aside to let them go through the doorway first: Chaves and Triste went down an impeccably polished wooden stairway into a kind of amphitheatre, with rows of seats stretching out in front of them and a long table draped with a red cloth, while behind them Kromer locked what, from where they were now standing, had become the exit: on one side of the table was the Argentine flag on a pole: on the other side, a projection screen mounted on a stand barely concealed another flag in whose centre, despite the folds, a swastika was visible: through some curtains concealing another entrance directly facing the stairway came a man dressed in the same unidentifiable uniform as that worn by Kromer: he was a tall man, with a white crew-cut and compact moustache, also white: he strode across the room towards Chaves, his outstretched arms making it clear an embrace was in the offing: when he got to him, he clasped him to his bosom with the words, "Father Chaves, how delightful to see you again": "and the gentleman here must be Señor Artola, is that right?": "indeed," said Triste for the second time, confirming his identity for the benefit of this new personage: "I'm Major Mendoza," the man who was obviously the boss introduced himself: "Father Chaves' Pope," thought Cristóbal

the first half hour was spent passing the time of day: pleasant tittle-tattle about this and that, without getting down to anything: Chaves and Major Mendoza did most of the talking; Triste kept a prudent silence and observed the Pope at his leisure: what army was he a major in? the Argentine army? some private army? or no army at all perhaps? as time went by, the conversation started to take a strange turn: they were engrossed in discussing God, the soul, salvation, the Church: suddenly, imperiously, the Major stood up and said, "let's get down to business," at the same time making an incomprehensible signal to Kromer, who had appeared through the curtains: "immediately, sir," Kromer acknowledged: swiftly and surely he went through all the necessary motions: with a swiftness and sureness born of practice, he whipped the red cloth off the table, went out of the room with it and seconds later came back in, wheeling a trolley with a large chest on it: out of the chest he first of all lifted a crucifix of no mean size, and a block on which he proceeded to mount it on the table: then came sundry items which Triste had seen on his occasional brief prowls round churches, moved by curiosity but never emerging much the wiser, partly because he felt embarrassed to ask, partly because he preferred to remain in the dark about such apparently transcendental matters

what Kromer was setting up on the table - lace cloth and silver utensils - was an altar: Chaves left the room through the curtains and came back a few minutes later in his priest's vestments: he took Major Mendoza by the arm and lovingly steered him to the far corner of the room, where a chair had been set out: he sat on it and signalled to the Major to kneel at his side so that, by slightly bowing his head, he could place his ear next to the other's mouth: presumably he was listening to his confession: Triste couldn't make head or tail of the muttered exchanges between his boss and his boss's boss, their roles suddenly reversed through that act of grace: the parley between the two men went on and on: by the time Chaves raised his hand to grant his penitent absolution, a good forty minutes had gone by: the Major stood up only to kneel down again behind the last row of seats, his eyes still lowered: Chaves, with beads of sweat on his forehead, went over to Kromer, who was standing beside the altar, and whispered something in his ear: Kromer went out, after nodding assent to Chaves, and came back almost immediately with a white cardboard box, which he held open so the priest could take out of it, putting them on as he did so, the garments needed to complete his sacramental attire: he then went to stand before the altar and, after a series of movements that meant nothing to Triste, leaning against the wall under the stairway, burst into Latin: Major Mendoza followed the ceremony dutifully and knowingly: the thought crossed Cristóbal's mind that perhaps he ought to copy his gesticulations so as to cover up his ignorance, but he concluded it was more respectful to follow the man's gestures and prayers from a standing position: at one point the Major walked to the altar, knelt before it, right in front of Chaves, his eyes raised to the heavens and mouth open, took communion and went back to his place: Triste supposed that the mass was nearly over but stayed where he was, hoping to receive instructions: the minutes went by incredibly slowly: finally he spotted certain gestures suggesting the end was in sight: Mendoza stood up and Chaves went out through the curtains, returning shortly after in his civilian clothes: "this way, Señor Artola," the Major said politely, "let's have have a little talk over a bite to eat"; Triste discovered what was behind the curtains: a corridor lined with locked glass cases led into another spacious room, where a table laid for three was waiting: Kromer's functions included those of cook and waiter: he executed both faultlessly: in the course of the meal the Major was to explain: "my dear Kromer, I got him out of Germany just before we lost the war, fixed him up with Argentine identity papers and took him on in my employ: I've never regretted it: he's superlative at everything he turns his hand to": Cristóbal couldn't help wondering what that "everything" included

"and you, Señor Artola, are you not a believer?" Mendoza inquired: "I don't know, I didn't get a religious education, Major": "that's something our good friend Chaves here should see to: religion is important, it brings such great rewards: you can't imagine how wonderful it is to know one is in a state of grace: I'd go to mass every day if I could leave this place; but as things are at present the most I can do is take a stroll in the garden at night, with all the house lights switched off, to get a breath of fresh air: I don't know what would become of my soul without Father Chaves' visits": "you exaggerate, Major," Chaves grovelled, "you'd go straight to heaven with or without a priest to assist you: just look at your confessions: a child has more sins to his name": so ran the conversation over lunch: Triste couldn't wait to get out of that bunker, that sunken amphitheatre, Kromer and his black shirt, Major Mendoza and his unctuous treatment of Chaves: he was tired and scared: scared of that place and those men, scared for reasons he could not fathom: he was in their service and received payment in return, but he dimly sensed that they were his enemies: only an enemy could call him "Señor Artola", with a deference that was a cover, a blatant cover, for revulsion at his origins and function: he felt better when Mendoza met him head on - that at least was more honest - with a question to which he did not have a clear-cut answer: "Chaves tells me," with the change of subject he was no longer Father Chaves, "you have no objection to killing people": "that depends," Triste responded: "depends on what?": "on the candidate - I wouldn't like to kill just anyone": "and what are your criteria, Señor Artola?": "I don't know, I wouldn't like to kill someone who was innocent": "only people who are guilty then ...": "that's right: only people who are guilty": "guilty of what?": "and ... communists, right? enemies ...": "enemies of yours, Señor Artola?": "that's just it, that's what I'd like to know, Major: so far the candidates I've been offered have been enemies of yours; what I'd like to know is whether my enemies are the same thing as your enemies": "as for that, Chaves will have explained to you, probably more than once, that our enemies are everyone's enemies, the enemies of society": Triste brought the conversation to a halt with his frank reply: "the thing is, I don't know if I'm the same thing as society, Major; in fact I'll go even further: I don't think I am"

as they were ushered out of the house by the ubiquitous Kromer, it was already getting dark: Triste still had no idea why he'd been summoned: he voiced his doubts to Chaves: "would you care to tell me just what the two of us came here for?": "that's obvious: me, to say mass; you, so the boss could get to know you": "and why should the boss want to get to know me? hasn't he got enough to do giving the orders?": "no, that's not enough for him: he wants to know who he's giving the orders to, if he's giving them to someone capable of carrying them out; and he wants to know who he's paying": "I thought we were going to meet another priest, one higher up than you: the Pope or something: and you give me an army man": "the relationship between the cross and the sword, Triste, is a long and happy one": "but I'm the one who wields the sword in this business, not him": "that's because he can't leave the house at present: later on he will, when things change: he's a great man, he could become president one day": "but right now he's not doing too well": "that's just temporary: these are difficult times and we can't put people like him at risk": "so that's why you go to give him your blessing?": "of course"

they didn't speak for the rest of the journey, each lost in their individual thoughts: they had just got out of the train when Triste said, "Chaves, do you believe all that crap, or are you doing it for the money, like me?": "and are you so sure, Triste, that you're only doing it for the money?": they walked in silence to the taxi rank: there they said goodbye and each took a separate cab: "corner of Avenida de Mayo and Salta," Triste gave instructions: he'd walk the few remaining blocks to Simón's café: not the Pope after all, Triste was thinking, but some sort of military man, and yet he's not the big chief, there are others above him: president, he thought, that loony? when Simón asked him how things were going, he replied: "fine, as always, what made you ask?"

Chapter 13. The Masses

That its sovereignty prolonged the light
my need believed and wrote in sand;
but night on lily toes came and
let loose its riders' rule of might.
LEOPOLDO MARECHAL, *On Night*

in early May 1965, just after the invasion of the Dominican Republic by United States Marines, Miguel Angel Zavala Ortiz, the then Argentine Foreign Secretary - and, ten years before, one of those bomber pilots Triste had seen in action over the Plaza de Mayo - triggered off one of the biggest manifestations of public outrage ever provoked by a government minister in the whole of the past 150 years since independence, by announcing that, with the backing of the military Supreme Command, he was sending troops to the Caribbean to support those sent by the United States: in the end the troops were never sent but, in bowing to mass public opinion over the issue of the nation's involvement in the predatory activities of a greater power, President Illia set in motion the train of events that would lead to his overthrow in a military coup some fourteen months later

Triste's part in the affair was purely peripheral: Chaves simply instructed him to keep an eye on things and, on the day of the mass rally in Plaza del Congreso, which exceeded the wildest expectations (with the demonstrators jamming the whole of the central square and overflowing to occupy an area stretching for at least twelve streets, packing Callao, Entre Ríos and Avenida de Mayo), ordered him to attend, armed, and if he got a chance, either from the cover of a doorway or from a safe distance at the top of the central steps up to the parliamentary building, to fire a couple of shots into the air to make people panic and stampede backwards or forwards, so that any fatal casualties would be the result of the crowd getting out of control, not of direct aggression: Cristóbal showed up as instructed, arriving well before the demonstration got under way: but from the word go he realized there was nothing to be done there with a pistol, unless he felt like shooting into the crowd pointblank, with the corresponding risk of being lynched: the boy he had worked with on the previous operations organized by Chaves, known to him as Héctor (who next day's papers would inform him was really called Héctor), turned up with exactly the same instructions: but his assessment of the situation was less acute than that of his fellow recruit: he too realized there was no way he could fire into the air and escape detection, but he did not rule out the option of firing straight into the surrounding crowd: for the moment, however, he did nothing: or rather, he held off, waiting for the right moment, when the crowd started to get restive, or when he had simply had enough and felt like going home: he forgot to take into account the degree of organization that must have gone into such a huge rally: he forgot to take into account the fact that the political parties who had called the rally, some legal, others not, were bound to have their own vigilantes stationed in the vicinity: he forgot to take into account the strength of the trade unions, whose security men were old hands at the business: he forgot to take any of those things into account because he had no political experience to draw on: and, unlike Triste, he was driven by emotion, by an unfocussed hatred, a passionate loathing for all mass events, for everything that for him smacked of the Left (which umbrella included practically every area of the political spectrum to the left of his own position, that is, practically every area of the political spectrum), for those who, despite his own pigmentation, he called "the blacks": he wasn't an idealist in Chaves' sense of the word, Chaves would never have called him that: he did the job for money, but there were occasions when he achieved that sublime fusion so many artists have striven for: the fusion in the same activity of work and pleasure: he was paid to kill, but he didn't kill only for the money but because killing gave him occasional moments of ecstasy: on that particular occasion he would get out his pistol and fire, not because he had been given orders but because he had been given the opportunity: in short, he was accountable to no one for such an action, no one - and no one here meant Chaves - would take him to task for it, nor was there any reason to suppose anyone would find out what he had done: so he bided his time waiting for his chance, or what he thought was his chance, to come

Triste paced up and down as if measuring, with necessarily restricted strides, the area of tarmac covered by the crowd: twice he left the assembled gathering - a densely packed, slow moving throng that reminded him, despite the shouting (of which there had been none on the previous occasion) of the densely packed, slow moving mass of mourners queuing to see Eva Perón's incorruptible body - in search of some side-street café where he could have a piss and a gin and, why not, think about his mother, his present, his bizarre future, if he had such a thing: it was as he came back to the square for the second time, yet again jostled by the crowd, his hand cupped round the pistol in his pocket to shield it and avoid attracting attention, yet again pushing his way through the crush, this time with the firm intention of crossing the square to the Congress Building and then carrying on up Rivadavia to find a quiet restaurant where he could get a meal before his last stop-off of the day, his friend Castro's café: it was on this second incursion into the thick of the crowd that, over and above the slogans chanted by all and sundry, over and above the interminable drone of the various speakers who despite the loudspeakers were inaudible, over and above his own desire to end his patrol uneventfully, without complicating his life or that of Chaves, over and above his will, in a nutshell, there rang out loud and clear - as clear as a shot - the sound of a pistol going off, followed almost immediately by a second report: Triste did not know at the time, nor at the time of events shortly after - he would find out only the following morning, when he scoured the papers cover to cover in an attempt to work out what had happened, to verify his suspicions - that in a corner of the square right next to the point he was heading for, near Rivadavia, a .38 bullet had cut short the life of a second-year medical student by the name of Daniel Grimbank, just twenty years old: Triste instinctively looked at his watch when he heard the second shot: it was exactly nine o'clock

a few seconds before nine o'clock Héctor, who was getting fed up and wanted to call it a day, though not without leaving some trace of his presence in the square, found himself close to the north-eastern edge of the demonst- ration, which petered out almost as soon as it got to Rivadavia, although it stretched another two or three blocks further down Callao: he decided to fire from the small clearing where he was standing: not simply pointblank but raising the gun to head level: he got out his pistol and, brandishing it, raised his outstretched arm, pressed the trigger, pressed it again, lowered his arm on seeing someone fall to the ground, covered in blood, just in front of him: he was sticking the .38 in his belt when some brawny arms clamped round him from behind, lifted him clear of the ground, and carried him off into Rivadavia, to the north side of the steps round the parliamentary building, where they hurled him to the ground: in the course of the short journey, the owner of the arms had been joined by several more men, a tough-looking bunch who, when his body hit the ground, closed round it, completely hiding it from view: behind them, more men clustered round in a protective cordon: they started to beat him up, some with their bare fists, other with sawn-off chains, others with knuckle-dusters, yet others with improvized truncheons made of strong cloth bags filled with metal nuts: they smashed not just his face: they smashed his whole body, kicking his knees and ankles, thrashing him in the ribs, the liver, the neck: just before losing consciousness, he knew it was the end

Triste fought his way as best he could through the crowd, which was now in a less compliant mood, scared by the two shots and by something that was going on out of view but close at hand: it was at that point, where the crowd thinned, that the fear was greatest, that there was the most unrest and commotion: nonetheless Cristóbal managed to get through to the clearing where the student, bathed in blood, lay on the ground and towards which were rushing the screeching sirens of a police car followed by an ambulance: Cristóbal looked at the corpse - he did not for a minute doubt that it was a corpse - and his attention was immediately drawn to the smaller crowd over by the steps: something was going on there that was bound to be of interest to him, so he rushed over : perhaps because of the determination with which he ran up, the men opened up a space to let him through and he was able to see his colleague's familiar body lying on the ground, by now reduced to a formless pulp: there were just enough distinguishing features left beneath the mask of blood and raw flesh for him to recognize him: he then looked around and realized that they were members of some security corps, whether belonging to a political party or trade union he did not care to find out right then, and that the best thing he could do to save his skin was to clear out, before they put two and two together and connected him with the human remains lying on the pavement: it was not difficult: the ever louder sound of sirens whose job it was to remind those who needed reminding of the existence of such things as storm troops and special state security forces caused the automatic, silent and unbelievably rapid break-up of the whole gathering, Triste included: the dying Héctor (in hospital he would hover between life and death for some days more, finally ceding defeat) was left behind, a battered body, waiting, his debts cancelled

Triste did not alter his plans: he walked to Once and went into the Rubí Pizzeria, on the corner of Rivadavia and Pueyrredón, facing the square with the controversial historical figure's mausoleum: he ate his meal calmly and took his time to empty the bottle of wine: it was half past ten when he went out into the street, walked to the corner and there hailed a cab to take him to the centre: "to Mitre and Callao," he said coolly: he wanted to know how things had ended: the bodies had been removed and the only people in sight were mounted police and the odd bewildered pedestrian crossing the avenue or scuttling along the pavement past the Congress Building: the silence was still heavy with shouting and shots, slogans and insults, but no one seemed to hear them: Triste slowly made his way down Avenida de Mayo to Salta, bound for Castro's café: it was as he got to the first crossing that he had his first vision: galloping up from the Plaza de Mayo towards him came a horse: on its back was a man with flowing hair and a beard - Triste would only discover two years later, on seeing the photograph of his corpse, taken in Camirí, on the cover of the magazine *Así*, that it was Che Guevara - with a machine gun in his raised right hand: the horse, which he had seen dozens of times before on countless posters, was Perón's pinto Spot: as he rode past Triste, the horseman leaned forward and, lowering his head to meet that of the rapt onlooker, shouted, "*Patria o Muerte!*": Cristóbal didn't get a chance to reply to the phrase or slogan or manifesto: he turned round to watch rider and steed sail off into the sky, disappearing over the statue of The Thinker, a Rodin obscured by the urban bustle and general ignorance: Triste instantly realized, by the expression on the faces of those around him, that only he had seen the strange individual on the general's horse gallop past at breakneck speed: he kept on walking without trying to enter into any communication with his blind, deaf and dumb fellow-citizens, who could let such extraordinary happenings pass them by

"what happened, then?", Chaves asked next day: "do you need me to tell you?" - by this time Triste had read everything there was to be read, and was not to be caught off his guard: "no, you needn't say a word; I know all about it: I was just asking for the sake of it": "if you want to know what I did, I can tell you: nothing, absolutely nothing: and if I had done anything, I'd have been a dead duck, like our Héctor: that lot meant business": "I know; dreadful, isn't it?": "what's so dreadful about it, Chaves? people have to defend themselves, don't they? do you expect them to wait for us to come and pump a few bullets into them, and say thank you into the bargain? not on your life: they'll defend themselves, and wouldn't you?": "what I'd do is shoot the lot of them, without bothering my head about things like that: they're all commies, the bastards; and the one who got killed was a Jew, did you know that?": "he didn't get killed: Héctor killed him, with your connivance and I'd even say your blessing, if that weren't treading on your professional toes - because all these political assassinations are just a hobby for you: what matters to you is your spiritual life in the Church's loving bosom, isn't it, Chaves? your man killed him, and I don't give a damn if he was Jewish: you can stop trying to sell me that one, because I won't buy: you can give all that crap to the boss, with his German flunkey and his little flags propped up behind your altar: he's the one who's bugged by Jews, not me": Triste was increasingly gaining ascendancy over Chaves: the priest seemed to like being treated with a scorn that was every day greater and less concealed: that fitted the self-image he was starting to acquire better than the respectful, subservient attitude he had preferred in the early days: "Chaves, tell me something," Triste asked, changing the subject and testing his strength, "do you ever fuck? do you take all that priest business seriously, or do you have a little bit on the side every now and then?": the priest stared at him, saying nothing, digesting the question, till tears welled up in his eyes: "what did you ask me that for, Triste? hadn't you realized I like boys? are you trying to humiliate me?": "no, Chaves: I never wanted to humiliate you, and it never occurred to me you didn't like women; sorry I asked, I meant it quite seriously, thinking just that: that every now and then you got yourself a girl": "no, women don't appeal to me, Cristóbal," and the tears went on streaming down his face: "there, there, Padre; we've all got our weaknesses, haven't we?: I've got my weaknesses too, so that makes two of us: both of us, guys with weaknesses: I go for something different but it all comes down to the same thing, doesn't it? weaknesses: we're both in the same boat, Chaves": and Chaves realized he was no longer boss

Book II
Counter-Tango

That affront, the tango, that blast
The treadmill of the years disdains;
Made of dust and time, men last
Less than its sparkling strains.

Time incarnate. The tango is the recall
Of a false past that cannot be denied,
The impossible memory of having died
By the knife, in some backstreet brawl.

JORGE LUIS BORGES,
The Tango

Chapter 14. University Life

It is impossible to describe ... the breakdown
of law and order in Buenos Aires following the
liberating army's retreat ... No one was safe
anywhere
JOSÉ MÁRMOL, *Amalia*

in the absence of more precise definitions, of explicit
political platforms making clear the differences between rival
groups - only by reading in between the lines could one
deduce certain tendencies: often crossing group boundaries,
and inconsistent with other tendencies shared by the same
group - in the absence, since 1962 and for many years to
come, of serious political analysis, it was commonly held that
the Argentine army was divided into two factions designated,
as with the parties of Byzantium, by a colour rather than a
name: Blues and Reds were divided by their conflicting views
as to the nature of the military coup both were plotting: with
the fall of the elected President Arturo Frondizi, the Blue
faction seemed to gain the upper hand, allowing the
President of the Senate to retain a semblance of legality and
call elections which, with both the Peronists and Communists banned, led to Arturo Illia's victory: nonetheless it was
an equally Blue general, Juan Carlos Onganía, who over-
threw the old doctor from Córdoba, a living example of civic
virtue who, when physically removed from his seat of office
by an army major who grabbed him by the ears, left the
Presidential Palace on foot, hailing a taxi to take him to his
private residence: one Blue military coup had succeeded
another, and the Communists said things could have been
worse, what would have been dreadful, really dreadful, would
have been a Red coup: Perón, from his Madrid exile,
recommended his supporters to "unsaddle their horses till
the situation became clearer", since Onganía was a decent

army chap and ought to be given a chance: it did not occur to Perón, himself an overthrown president, to criticize the overthrow of another president: he was less of a president than a general: a Blue general, so it seemed, who was condoning a Blue coup: the true-blue events that followed the Blue coup were enough to undermine the most masochistic fantasies about what might have happened if the coup had been a Red one: could the Reds have done anything worse? was their Right to the right of the Blue Right? who knows? would Perón have given the same horsemanly advice if it had been a decent Red army chap? who knows? Triste did not bother himself with such matters: what mattered to him was how things would affect him, whether there would be the same demand for his labours under the new regime, what kind of deal with the latter might have been struck by Major Mendoza or whoever backed him with cash, now tripled with inflation (Triste's salary currently stood at ninety thousand pesos), whether his relationship with his unknown employers might be terminated, leaving him without a job

"don't worry, Triste," Chaves reassured him, "this lot are less concerned with making than breaking: and breaking is what we're here for: they'll be calling on our services in no time at all, you'll see": and so indeed they did, just twenty-four hours after Onganía's installation in the Casa Rosada as President of the Republic: "of what republic, that's what I'd like to know," a client in Simón Castro's café asked, "when they've suspended the constitution?": "I'd keep your objections to yourself, if I were you," Cristóbal recommended, "you never know who might be listening": Chaves brought the order: "we've got to go and stir things up a bit at the University": and off Triste went to fire some shots in the air to cause a disturbance and set people running, so that the storm troops, who at the time were taking over official control from the University authorities, could move in: the Infantry sergeant who led the troops into the Faculty of Science did so, as if testifying to the incredible ignorance of those who wielded power, to the cry, "down with university autogeny": he shouted the word "University" with a small "u", just as Chaves had muttered the word "University" with a small "u": and the reference to autonomy was just his way of justifying the view that education comes out of the barrel of a gun, though he did not say it in so many words: "down with university autogeny," and they charged in wrecking everything, undoing the work of years, and that was just the start, the prologue to the far more serious, definitive, irreversible undoing that would reach a climax ten years later, in 1976: "down with university autogeny," and Triste fired in the air and General Imaz, speaking on behalf of the Government, told the press that Argentina was a Western nation, whose structures, way of life and mentality were entirely Western, and Triste fired in the air again, and the general came out cleanly and openly against all "Oriental political doctrines", and the reporters jotted his comments down and published them without daring to put a *sic* in brackets after the bit about "Oriental political doctrines", but the [*sic*] was understood by everybody, and Triste realized that from now on there was going to be plenty of work for him and the best thing he could do was ask for more pay , and he fired in the air again, as everyone was streaming out of the Faculty building, just before Chaves came up to him and pointed to a very tall, fair-haired young man, and said, "see that one over there, the tall one with the fair hair?": "yes": "he's to be eliminated": and Triste closed one eye and stretched out his arm, aiming his pistol at his head: "no, you blockhead, not here," the priest shrieked just in time: "too bad," Cristóbal thought as he lowered his hand: "too bad, we're going to have do it in cold blood, at night, with no one around: that's just too bad": "I'll tell you how it's got to be done later," Chaves promised, "as for now, let's clear out of here": they bolted up the deserted, broad white stairs and then up the concealed, rusty fire escape out on to the roof, the open air, and some unsuspected exit into a backstreet

"Starobinsky," Chaves said: "his name's Starobinsky, a genius at maths, a Jew and a commie": "cut it out, Chaves, I don't want to know: so he's brilliant with numbers? that makes me kind of take to him: I can still shoot him, but I'm kind of taking to him: if you tell me anything else, what sort of a mother he's got, that his girlfriend's tall and lanky like him, that he plays the piano, then I'll start to get to know him, I'll take to him even more and I won't be able to press the trigger, see?": "OK: then I'll just tell you where he lives, what time he usually comes home, where you're to wait for him, where you're to kill him: we've rented a house": "we've what?": "we've rented a house on the corner of his street: you're not to shoot from the street: you're to shoot from inside the house, with the lights out: it's a corner house, with two exits: you go in one and come out of the other": "and who's rented the house?": "someone with a false name and false papers, someone who's not going to be seen again: here's the key": "so I arrive after dark, go into the house, shoot him from a window overlooking the street, what street?": "Calle Yerbal": "overlooking Calle Yerbal, with a silencer so as not to cause too much of a disturbance, and then I beat it out of the door to ... what's the name of the other street?": "I can't remember, I'll tell you later": "everything thought out, planned, set up for me: and for Starobinsky": "how about tomorrow?": "fine, the sooner the better": "you get a bonus, here, fifty thousand": "a kind of Christmas box, is that it, for dispatching Starobinsky? what's he done to upset them, Chaves?": "he's a student leader, I think: a troublemaker who needs getting out of the way": "if I didn't know what kind of a priest you are, I'd ask you to say a prayer for him and for me; but your prayers can't have a lot of influence up there": "don't be so sure, Triste, I'm a believer": "and you say your prayers just in case...": Triste had never heard of Pascal's wager: he left Chaves sitting at the table in the Tortoni and went out into the cold outside: they're out of their minds if they think that's how I'm going to do it, from a safe distance, like being at a rifle range: if it's a corpse they want, they can have it, but I'll do it my way

at seven o'clock, when night had already fallen on the sluggish, clinging Buenos Aires winter, Triste was briskly walking the streets round Parque Lezama: he turned down a particularly dark street off Balcarce, made sure that no one was in sight, that there was no one hidden in some doorway watching him, and tried the door of the first parked car he got to before realizing it wasn't the kind of car he needed: the third car was a new, black model: he walked up to it confidently, and fiddled with the lock for a few seconds, with the aid of a special contrivance: he got in and sat at the wheel: leaning forward, he felt for the wires under the dashboard and started up the engine: he did everything quite calmly, as if he'd been doing it all his life: with a touch of sadness, perhaps: he drove slowly, crossing the city first to the north, then to the west, looking for Calle Yerbal: while stopped at some traffic lights, he took his pistol out of his pocket and laid it on the seat beside him: he finally got to Starobinsky's corner and turned into the street, parking about a hundred yards from the house to which the student was to return: he glanced up at the house on the corner, whose keys he had in his pocket, and grinned, thinking what heavy weather the experts make of things: the more of an expert you become, the more you complicate things for yourself: a lease signed by someone who might be recognized, false papers, unnecessary rental payments, conversations, clues, dozens of pointless clues, just to avoid facing up to a simple fact: that one man can kill another with no more help than a jackass's jawbone: it struck eight: Triste kept the engine running and the lights off: a couple walked past deep in conversation, then an old lady, hobbling slowly, who peered into the sedan: Triste turned his head away from the pavement, avoiding her prying eyes: at half past eight he saw his man, walking towards him with no idea of what was about to happen to him: twenty seconds later, Triste got out of the car, leaving the door open: from over the car roof he watched Starobinsky walk nearer and nearer, while he put the silencer on his pistol: when the young man was about ten yards away, Triste walked round the front of the car and stood in his path, forcing him to look up: two yards away from his killer, he halted: "good evening," said Triste, giving him time for the truth to dawn as he raised the arm with the gun and aimed it at his forehead: "what do you...?" Starobinsky tried to ask: a strange sound, from the silencer, a kind of slurp, and a round, red hole, dark red, between his eyebrows before he fell to the ground, in slow motion, keeling over, collapsing like a pack of cards, without completely abandoning an upright position till it was all over and he lay grotesquely spread-eagled beneath a trenchcoat just like that of Chaves, except that it covered the prone body of a mathematician and not the still-erect body of a murderer: Triste waited till Starobinsky was flat on the ground, at his feet: there was no one around: pointing the barrel of the gun downwards, he fired at the back of his head: another slurp, another perfect circle: calmly he went back to the car and cruised off, picking up speed as he went on: he hit a main road and turned right into it, looking for a poorly-lit side street: he found one almost immediately, turned off and parked about eighty yards down the street: he got out, went back to the well-lit avenue he had just left and immediately hailed a cab: "Pueyrredón and Sarmiento," he said: when he got there he went into the first bar he saw: he had a gin and went back outside: he walked in the direction of Once Station till he found another cab: "Avenida de Mayo and Salta," he instructed the driver "he was wearing a trenchcoat just like yours: the idea even went through my head that it was you I'd killed: only for a split second, but the idea occurred to me," was all he said to Chaves before handing back the keys to the house, without further comment: what was the point of saying anything about the stupidity of all those preliminary arrangements? who was he going to convince that you either kill a man looking him in the eye or you don't kill him? especially since it probably wasn't true: there must be men capable of shooting another man in the back in cold blood: the man who dreamt up the idea of the house, the idea of death from a window, must be a man like that: and he hadn't even thought of fixing a getaway car: he'd still have been wandering the streets, Triste thought: that night he slept badly, he dreamt of Chaves with a dark red, round hole in the middle of his forehead: he woke up in a cold sweat and opened the bedside-table drawer where he no longer hid his savings but his weapons, his two weapons, he whipped it out in a panic to check the pistols were still there: he looked at himself in the mirror his mother had hung on the wall so many years before, had a drink of water and a big swig of gin and went back to sleep: again he dreamt of Chaves, of the back of Starobinsky's head, of the rider shouting, shouting just for his benefit, "*Patria o Muerte!*": and he was whispering to Chaves, "*Patria o Muerte!* Padre": and the priest was pointing to the student's lifeless body: at five in the morning, Doña Amanda's screams definitively plucked him from his tormented half-sleep: "Cristóbal," the old woman was hysterical, "Cristóbal, help...": and Triste rushed out into the freezing yard without flinging any clothes on and the old woman grabbed him fiercely by the hand, as if to stop him turning back: "help, help," she screamed and wouldn't let go till he was inside Fernando's room, Don Fernando, old Fernando, his friend Fernando, sitting in his chair, immobile, already rigid, his arms on the table propping him up, his staring eyes trained on the door, his mouth twisted, having succumbed to the irremediably empty death of the lonely: Triste grabbed some clothes and went to get the doctor: authorized to practice or not, Don Matías signed the death certificate: then he rang the undertaker's and, as they waited for the men to arrive with the coffin, he carefully took a tiny key off his key ring: he opened the wardrobe and from the back of it produced a box, the box to which he had the key: he opened it in front of Doña Amanda and Triste: it was full of money: five hundred, six hundred thousand pesos, Cristóbal calculated: "this is yours, Amanda: that was his wish: you're to pay for the funeral out of it, and the rest... you can do what you like with it": that was all the doctor said: "Doña Amanda," Triste wanted to know, "how come you found him at this time of night?": "I'd been coming to his room of late to sleep with him on cold winter nights: neither of us liked sleeping alone": Triste didn't open his mouth again till it was all over and they came out of the cemetery, leaving Fernando in his grave: before going home he looked for a call box and rang Simón Castro: "Simón, can you find your way to my house?... yes, I know you brought me home drunk a couple of times, but it's complicated... fine: hire a car or a van and be here in two hours' time, OK? no, there's nothing serious up: I'm moving": Castro turned up punctually: Cristóbal had packed all his belongings in two suitcases bought in Malena's time, bought precisely for that purpose, and in the old suitcase she had left behind, which he hadn't liked to throw out: exhausted by the sleepless night and the trip to the cemetery, Doña Amanda was fast asleep when he took his things out of the room and piled them into the car his friend had brought: "I'll leave the cases at your café and find myself someplace to live": they had nearly got to the end of their journey when Castro, out of curiosity, asked him to explain his reasons: "everything in that place smells of death," Triste said, "I'd better clear out now, or I'll be the only one left": the only one left was Doña Amanda, left in the rambling, empty house, with no one to huddle up to in that bitter winter: a week later Castro, who read the papers from cover to cover, pointed out the news: old lady gassed by fumes from brazier or something like that, Doña Amanda asphyxiated, lifeless, blue: "suicide," was Triste's verdict

Chapter 15. Revenge

You will be the last woman in my life
my tiny Cristina ...
ROQUE DALTON, *Promises*

Starobinsky had been a start, just a start: soon there would be new offers, new handsome rewards: orders, payments: Chaves was going to pieces: from the moment Triste had made it clear they were both in the same boat, that there were no more distinctions, there was no more authority, that they were accomplices to a common crime, the priest started to go downhill, to lose his nerve, his energy, his senses: as far as the money was concerned he began to be a mere go-between, and in practical matters a mere assistant: he had things to learn from Triste, and he lacked certain things that Triste had and he would never have: things took a turn for the worse when Major Mendoza (Triste supposed, largely rightly, that he was Chaves' only permanent link with the leaders of the nameless organization they worked for: so nameless that no one had ever talked of the existence of an organization, so unknown and remote it was barely conceivable that a grassroots recruitment officer like Chaves might know anyone else: which did not prevent a large number of people at the top, at the very top, from knowing all there was to know about the priest and Triste) ordered a new assassination: Triste, Chaves and however many assistants might be needed were to put a violent end to the existence of an individual by the name of Wilson Nerva, a subversive element, etc., according to the description Chaves tried to slip in by way of a preface: "cut it out, Chaves, I told you months ago: if something's got to be done, it'll be done, but don't try and make out we're the exclusive agents of good in Argentine society: don't try and tell me the guy's a commie, a Jew, an agitator: the most you need to say about a guy with a name like that is he's Uruguayan: then we might understand one another: you turn up and say: Triste, we've got to get rid of a Uruguayan: I'm not going to ask you the reason why: because they beat us at football, because he's the president's wife's lover, just because: but don't tell me he's a monster because there are laws to deal with monsters and that's no reason to pack him off him with a one-way ticket: all you have to do is go to the police and say: Wilson Nerva's a monster: he wets his bed at the age of forty, he's having it off with his granny from Paysandú and he's a member of some illegal party or other - whichever party bugs you the most - and they'll ask you which party? make a note of it and stick him in the clink for the rest of his days": "but Triste, do you think we haven't got enemies?": "we? and who's we? Major Mendoza's Nazis? Kromer? the fatherland? you're off your rocker, Chaves: we don't have enemies: it's the guys who pay us who've got enemies: all we've got are friends, guys who pay us, and victims: and that's all there is to it: what have they tried to con you into believing about this guy, or what are you trying to con me into believing?": "that he's a subversive element, that he knows things about us that could make things tricky for us...": "and what can Wilson Nerva know about us, about you and me? the trouble is you can't see that when the bosses say 'us', they mean themselves: they say 'us' to involve us in their dirty work: apart from which, what you've just said they said to you: that's a threat, Chaves: either you wipe this guy out, or we let everything we know out of the bag: the two Jews, Starobinsky, your aunt's sister: they're threatening us, Chaves, and you just sit there meekly: who made the threat? Mendoza?": "yes, Mendoza": "because you're not in contact with anyone else, with anyone higher up": "there's ... well, no": "is there a reward?": "five hundred grand": "half a million? not bad": "so, the job's on?": "look, Chaves, I never said I wouldn't do it: all I said was that you didn't have to do the big sell, you didn't have to try and justify it: I knew before you started I was going to kill a guy who's worth more than me: he has to be worth more than me: the first one's a watchmaker and I'm a hired killer: he's worth more than me: the next one's a mathematician and I'm a hired killer: he's worth more than me: shall I go on with the list?": "no, forget it: but this one's different: he's liquidated more than a few in his time, he's no innocent": "and did he get paid for liquidating them, Chaves?": "no: his motives were political": "then he's worth more than me: that doesn't change anything: I'm going to get paid, I get paid, for pumping a few holes in him when I've got nothing personal against him, see?": "sure I do": "good"

but Chaves had to go into details: except that the details he had to give were true: their target belonged to a group, he explained, who were in the preliminary stages of planning an armed "people's revolution": "there's not all that many of them, but they don't all know each other, there are some recent recruits, internal disagreements: if this one can be got out of the way, his death can be nailed, hopefully literally, on one or other of his comrades: that way they'll wipe each other out within six months": "it's getting uglier and uglier, Chaves: now it's not enough to send someone packing and clear out of the picture: now we've got to drag others down into the muck: it's getting uglier and uglier": "let's stick to the facts, Triste: Wilson Nerva, a Uruguayan but who's lived in Buenos Aires since he was a boy, a defence lawyer specializing in lost causes, lives with a woman in an apartment rented in her name: he's only in partial hiding: he still goes to his office, to the law courts, he's still seen around: the building's on the corner of Jujuy and Hipólito Yrigoyen, in Once: the job involves hanging around, watching his regular movements, double-checking for possible errors: then it's a matter of entering the building, going up to his place, it's on the fourth floor, ringing the bell, waiting for him to come to the door, forcing the lock if he's asleep and doesn't hear": "a defence lawyer specializing in lost causes: Chaves, why do you always have to tell me things that make me start to like these guys? do you want me to feel sorry later? why do I have to keep killing people I'm starting to like? I really take to this one, Chaves: he sounds like a great guy, this Uruguayan of yours, so let's be quick about it, before I get to like him too much: better go and kill him right away": "Triste": "what, Padre?": "they want us to use machine guns, that's the thing: lots of noise, lots of blood, lots of bullets, lots of screaming: a public example: the splinter group, the rival faction want to leave no doubt about who's who in this fight to the death": "and just who are they, this splinter group?": "no idea, I've never set eyes on them, but we're to daub *MNR-mla* on the wall: *Movimiento Nacional Revolucionario (marxista-leninista auténtico)*: how about that?": "it makes me want to puke, Chaves; what I'd like to know is who's going to feel like painting anything on the wall when it's time to beat the hell out of the place": "I'll do the painting, Triste, I can do it in a flash: you can stand at the door with the machine gun to cover me": "and supposing the neighbours come out to see what's going on, to see what the row is about? am I supposed to do them in as well? after all ... one, two, three more ... makes no difference really: and you can go and hang around in the corner café if you like, watching his movements day in day out, for a month, pretending nothing funny's going on: who's the pisshead who thinks up these bright ideas? does he want us to end up in Devoto Jail or something? we do the job on the spot, without all that fuss and bother: would you recognize the guy?": "yes, I saw him once": "then we spend one day waiting for him: he's got to show up at some point: we let an hour or so go by, and in we go: right?": "whatever you say, Triste: this envelope's for you: it's got the five hundred grand in it; we'll do the job on Monday, OK?": "OK"

Triste spent the weekend getting hold of a car, spraying it a different colour and swapping the number plates for false ones: they weren't going to hang around in the café with the two machine guns on the table: a car was better, and there was parking space in Hipólito Yrigoyen; they'd have to be either the first or last parked car so they could make a quick getaway when it was all over: he also got hold of two different-looking, tough leather bags, one for each weapon, so they could put them in the car trunk and get them out when it was time to go into the building: on Sunday he went to bed late and slept till noon on Monday: at four he was in the Tortoni waiting for Chaves, who turned up half an hour later: he had already had two gins: the priest asked for a whisky, a double, neat: he knocked it back and, before the waiter had had time to turn away from the table, ordered a repeat: "feel better now, Chaves?" Triste asked, watching the colour come flooding into the priest's cheeks: "yes, that's better": "don't worry: we'll buy a bottle of gin to take with us in the car, how about that?": "what car, Triste?": "the car we're going to do the job in": "and where did you get it from?": "I stole it, resprayed it, changed its plates, OK?": "I suppose so": "don't suppose anything, Chaves: it's OK"

they bought the gin in a shop in Avenida de Mayo and took a taxi to fetch their own car, waiting in a lock-up on Constitución: Triste casually opened up the garage door, made Chaves wait outside, got the car out and, as Chaves climbed into the passenger seat, locked up and hid the key he had used in a crevice between two bricks in the flaking side wall next to the entrance: at a quarter past five they were parked at the front of the long row of cars lining the street: there was nothing ahead of them, and the apartment block where Wilson Nerva lived happened to be on the same side of the street: they wouldn't have to run across Jujuy to get to the car: they could drive straight off: it was starting to warm up (it was early spring 1967), but Chaves needed to keep drinking to steady his nerves: he was genuinely scared: all Triste was thinking about was how, supposing they found the guy asleep, he'd have to wake him up: he wasn't going to shoot anyone in the back: he had a few swigs of gin too: at ten thirty, Chaves said "that's him", clutching at Triste's arm: "that's Wilson Nerva": he was not alone

he was holding the woman tightly as if he sensed that she was the last woman in his life, that he was going to make love to her for the last time, that somewhere, in some unfathomable place, someone was keeping count of the last minutes of his life as they ticked away, suddenly acquiring a tragic urgency: they kissed before crossing the road and going into the building, brushing the back of the car whose occupants would, shortly after, break into his refuge, his bedroom, his sleep, spraying bullets right, left and centre, putting an end to his labours, his disappointments, his loves: putting an end not only to his existence but to what gave that existence meaning: dozens of men in prison, in hiding, out of action, wholly dependent on him, on his moral integrity, who would lose everything the minute he was violently removed from this world: his arm was still around the woman's shoulder as he went into the block and pressed the button to call the elevator: they went up to his apartment: both of them feeling the need to make love: the need, more than ever before, to be naked, to be together, to be one, to exist just for each other

Triste consulted his watch: it was ten forty and he decided to wait till eleven: he thought of Wilson Nerva walking around inside, going into the kitchen, making a cup of instant coffee, going to the toilet, getting undressed, undressing the woman, leaving his lit cigarette on the bedside table, forgotten: he took another swig of gin and wiped his mouth with his sleeve: "let's go," he said when his watch said eleven: he opened the trunk and signalled to Chaves to get out the bag that was his: inside it, apart from the machine-gun, was a tin of black paint, a thick brush, a pair of gloves: everything they needed to go upstairs and kill a man because they were being paid to do so, and a woman because she was there and had to share her lover's fate: Triste had no difficulty picking the lock of the door to the street and they went in: the elevator was desperately slow in getting them to the right floor: they got out: they pressed the doorbell, which rang loud and clear on the other side of the flimsy wooden door: "coming," said a man's voice, "I'm just coming": he opened the door just enough to stick his head round it, hiding his body behind the varnished surface that so ill protected him: he was naked: "who is it?" the woman asked from another room: "Wilson Nerva?" Triste said: "yes," the lawyer replied and saw death staring him in the face: Triste fired two rounds through the door: it was enough but he wanted to be quite sure, so he took one step inside and aimed at the ground, pumping another round into the bleeding, crumpled heap: Chaves stepped through the doorway behind him, just in time to intercept the woman as she came out of the bedroom, naked, a pistol in her hand: she had time to press the trigger once, to no effect, before Chaves riddled her with bullets: three rounds, fired not from left to right, right to left, but the full length of her body, from head to toe, toe to head, head to toe: and still, from the ground where she lay, she managed to shout, "*Patria o Muerte!*": Chaves didn't understand the words: he rushed into the bedroom and daubed the wall over the bed: *MNR-mla*: he painted the letters in the tiny kitchen too: "get out, Chaves," Triste said, "beat it": the elevator was waiting with the door open: no one came out to see what was happening they got into the car and Triste slammed his foot down on the accelerator: "that was lucky," said Chaves, "the neighbours didn't even stick their heads out": "what a load of motherfuckers," was Triste's response, "they haven't even got the guts to find out what's going on: what a fucking country, don't you think, Chaves?": "I don't know...": "yes, you do: you know all sorts of things: you know how to use a machine gun to perfection, you know how to paint lies on the wall, you know how to make them drop like ninepins to keep the money coming in: a model operation, it was: you've got something to boast about to Mendoza: but I know the truth about you, Padre: you were shit scared: whiter than the corpse: but I won't let on, you needn't worry: now you can tell me, how much cash did they give you for me?": "five hundred grand, Triste": "oh no they didn't, Padre: they gave you more than that: twice that? we've dispatched a real big shot, a key leader, an innocent, with no bodyguard and no safety precautions - just fancy opening the door like that - but a real big shot: tomorrow's papers will be full of the carnage: they gave you more cash than that, Chaves: tell me how much more": "it wasn't twice as much, Triste": "three quarters of a million?": "yes": "when can I have it?": "tomorrow": "do you know I nearly finished you off, Chaves? with the girl's pistol, when you were doing your painting: I didn't do it because you owed me money: next time you might not be so lucky": "I know I'm going to come to a sticky end, Triste: but I can't believe you hate me that much: there are others who...": "cut out the crap, Chaves": he parked the car carefully: the two men got out, each with his bag, his sinister tool kit: "you go that way," Triste said, "and I'll go this way, OK?": "as you like, Triste: but explain something to me: she said something when she was on the ground, didn't she?": "sure she did": "did you get what she said?": "sure, how could I not get it? *Patria o Muerte*, that's what she said, Chaves": "and what does that mean?": "beat it, Chaves, I'll see you tomorrow in the Tortoni": he walked a few yards and turned round to check the priest was going off in the other direction: he was near Spinetto Market: he smelt the usual market smells: smells of rotting food, of horse piss, fresh vegetables too: when he got to the market he took a deep breath and, turning to a drunk propped in a doorway with a bottle, shouted - a strangled, quavering shout, with a sob somewhere in its depths - shouted, "*Patria o Muerte!*" and kept on walking

Chapter 16. A Military Corpse

As the light of evening wanes
Sobbing in the western skies
A mournful shadow flies
Over Argentina's open plains.
RAFAEL OBLIGADO, *Santos Vega*

although the profession accorded Cristóbal Artola by life was concerned with death, his participation was not always confined to the forcible launch of souls into eternity to which circumstances and an innate lack of moral scruples had accustomed him: in mid-1970, in the heart of winter, round about the time of his birthday, he found himself involved in an assignment that was no less murderous but less hazardous and more bureaucratic: it was at that time that he transported and, some three hundred miles from Buenos Aires, buried an unidentified corpse which he would soon discover was that of an important personage: it was the body of General Pedro Eugenio Aramburu, a former national president from some fifteen years back who had given up his military post for politics, founding a parliamentary party to continue the fight in the civilian arena: there are conflicting versions of his kidnap and subsequent murder, some more far-fetched than others

(one such version, published as an official report by the journal *The Peronist Cause* some three years after the event, attributed responsibility to the armed wing of the Peronist Movement, the Montoneros: according to this account, a number of figures connected with the guerrilla organization, all dead by the time the report was published, were supposed to have kidnapped the general, subjected him to a "people's trial", found him guilty and sentenced him to death, subsequently "executing" him: the account was a full one, peppered with "authentic" touches flattering to victim and murderers alike: it was said, for example, that when preparing to meet his end Aramburu had had his shoes polished, a final gesture worthy of the upright soldier who does his duty to the last: it was also stated that, at the fateful hour, the general had taken it upon himself to resolve any remaining doubts, expressing his conformity with a virtual command: "you may proceed," he is alleged to have said, whereupon the execution followed suit: an admirable example of military rectitude on the part of the speaker, but also a recognition of his interlocutors' authority, a recognition of the legitimacy of the whole sequence of events leading to his death, a recognition of the existence of an enemy and consequently of a state of war, for it was indeed a war that was starting: a birth certificate validating the beginnings and status of a people's army, whose first major operation had been his own arrest and trial

(a second version, attested by Captain Aldo Luis Molinari of the Argentine Navy, a former Head of Police under Aramburu's presidency, suggests that the "disappeared" general was planning a would-be coup - "pro-democracy coup" was Molinari's term - against the Blue General Onganía: according to the naval officer, Onganía had had him kidnapped and then killed at the Military Hospital: if Molinari is to be believed, a group of armed men dragged Aramburu from his home and handed him over to another group in some corner of the extensive grounds of the Law Faculty: this second group took him to the Military Hospital, which he would leave a dead man: those who had taken him there or another group transported his body to the house of a man called Orué in Villa Domínico, on the outskirts of the capital: Orué passed the body on to Firmenich's men, who buried him in Timote: after the burial a chain of killings eliminated the whole of the original group of kidnappers, the same group who, in the Montonero - or simply Peronist

- version of events, were supposedly responsible also for his trial, sentence and execution: with their deaths no one was left to contradict the "official" report

(a third angle on events is provided by General Lanusse in his published memoirs of those bloody years, which claim that Aramburu was kidnapped by "a terrorist group made up of certain individuals of extreme right-wing persuasion": which in practice does not conflict with either of the previous accounts but offers a composite, complementary version: a composite version in the sense that what matters are not the details but the fact of the kidnap and its consequences: a complementary version because it specifies the political affiliation of the assailants, regardless of whether they were responsible for the whole sequence of events or simply for snatching the general from his home and handing him over to others)

Triste received a call from Chaves on the 29th May, a few hours after the kidnap, on the phone with which his new apartment was equipped: they had to meet right away, in the usual place: the Tortoni was deserted, which was unusual for that time of afternoon when the city's inhabitants take their siesta in the form of conversation, the animation of which belies its true function: "got a car we can use, Triste?" Chaves fired the question at him before he'd barely had a chance to sit down: "of course I've got one, I always have," Triste snapped edgily: "so now they've realized cars come in handy, have they? about time, I'd say": "a bit jumpy today, aren't we, Cristóbal? calm down, there's nothing big on: just a little liaison job that needs doing quickly by someone reliable: they know they can rely on us": "come on, Chaves: you told them we'd got the car before you'd even consulted me, didn't you? but of course we've got a car lined up, that's what you told them, isn't it?": "sure, Cristóbal": "see? that's what's making me jumpy: they don't think they can rely on us: they've no reason to rely on us: we're not the sort of people you rely on, that's the brutal truth; but you want them to rely on us, and you say yes to everything because you rely on me: and one fine day I'm going to let you down: not because I want to let you down, but because I can't foresee everything, I can't always have everything ready for any eventuality, come night or noon: look Chaves, they don't have to rely on us: they pay us, they keep us in the lap of luxury precisely because they can't rely on us: it's our ambition they're relying on, the fuel that drives the engine, not the engine itself: and fuel is what they've got: we provide the engine if we feel like it: we provide the engine if we're happy with the fuel: that's all there is to it; so don't give them the come on, don't commit yourself - and me into the bargain - before you know exactly how things stand: if we haven't got what they want, that's too bad: if we have got it, or they think we've got it because you told them so, and then we don't come up with the goods, and they think we're not coming up with the goods because we're doing the dirty on them, they won't think twice about it: they'll send over a couple of tough guys, tougher than the two of us put together, to sort us out, got it?": "OK, I've got it": "good: let's go and get the car, then: you can pay the taxi fare, serves you right for not using your head": they went outside and flagged down a cab: Cristóbal instructed the driver to take them to a backstreet out at Villa Ortúzar

Triste pulled the metal garage door to and, before getting into the driver's seat, put the key to the padlock in his pocket, a detail which did not escape Chaves' notice: "keep your questions to yourself, Chaves: I know what's going through your mind about the key and whether the garage is mine or not: that's my business": "I wasn't going to say a word, promise": "that's even worse: you'd noticed and you weren't going to say a word: that's worse still; right then, what happens now?": Triste had got as far as Federico

Lacroze, heading for Chacarita: "we've got to pick someone up at Tucumán and Suipacha: he'll be waiting for us on the corner in an hour's time": "an hour's time?": "right": "let's go for a drink then": he turned right, down a side street: a couple of minutes later they were cruising the residential streets, with plenty of parking spaces and antiquated taverns on the oldest corners: Triste switched the engine off twenty yards or so from one of those corners, which formed part of a now forgotten city, doomed to give way to the multi-storey blocks and motorways of the future, and they went into a bar: "a double gin, chilled and neat," Triste ordered the barman, turning to Chaves: "do you know the guy who's waiting for us?": "no, but he knows me": "how does he know you?": "I've no idea ... from a photo, I suppose": "that's what I was afraid of, from a photo: what photo, Chaves? have you ever given a signed photo of yourself to Major Mendoza so he can pray to it in his spare time? you haven't? well I haven't either: but they've got photos of us: we're working for the cops, but with the none of the advantages the cops have got: if we get caught, we pay for it like a couple of stooges, without being able to name any names or get bailed out by any of the motherfuckers we're working for: what a mess, Chaves; what a bloody mess": "I know all that: I've known it for ages but we're in it up to our necks now": "sure, but one day we're going to want out: and then what happens?": "I don't know what happens then": "you'd better start thinking about it, Chaves": they had another gin and went back to the car

at exactly half past six they reached the corner of Tucumán and Suipacha, where the flow of traffic made it impossible to stop for a minute without incurring the wrath of a hundred drivers: there was no need: a man in a trenchcoat just like the priest's, equally worn and superfluous, bent down to peer through the car window and, seeing the face he was looking for, came straight over to the back door and climbed into the seat behind Triste: "Chaves?" he inquired, proffering his right hand: "yes, that's me," the priest replied, responding to the newcomer's politeness with a smile and clasping the hand held out to him: "my name's Peñaloza," the man informed them, looking in Cristóbal's direction: the latter, who had observed every movement in the rearview mirror, did not take his hands off the wheel or look round: "they call me Triste": "pleased to meet you, Mr Triste," the man who went by the name of Peñaloza replied with a total lack of consideration or thought: "where are we to go?": "make for the Military Hospital": "OK": and they headed off without a further word interrupting the silent, steady drive: when they got to Avenida Luis María Campos, Triste observed: "we're nearly there, Peñaloza": "fine, turn in, make for the casualty department, the entrance signposted for ambulances": Triste obeyed: inside the gates they were stopped by a soldier: Peñaloza got out of the car and showed him some papers: the latter saluted and, as soon as Peñaloza had climbed back in, waved Triste on: they drove down into a vast underground area with several exits, which were presumably the transaction points for much of the hospital's business: there were various service elevators for collecting the laundry and the refuse from the kitchens and wards, and for delivering medicines, equipment and food: it was obviously also the collection point for the monstrous clinic's human refuse: one of the elevators - Triste knew instinctively which one - clearly led down from the morgue: "pull in over there: back the car up to that door: you haven't got anything in the trunk, have you? nothing that takes up space?": "the trunk of this car is one big, empty hole, Peñaloza: I don't use this car for holidays, you know": "I never imagined you did," the mysterious director of operations replied straight-faced: "are we going to be here long?": "I'll go in and see how things are getting on; I'll be back with instructions": Triste switched off the engine, lit up a cigarette, and settled back for a long wait: he was not mistaken: it was ten when

Peñaloza emerged from the elevator that led down from the morgue and motioned to him to open the trunk: Triste got out with the keys and did as he was told: out of the building came two men with a bulky object: clearly a human body in a big, black plastic bag: they put it in the trunk and helped Triste close up: "here," Peñaloza said: "this is the delivery address": it was an address in Villa Domínico, with a hand drawn map of how to get there from the station: "they'll wait up for you, no matter how late you get there: take it easy: there'll be no police checks and Avellaneda bridge will be open": "fine," Triste said and got back into the driving seat

they got to Villa Domínico at midnight and took some twenty minutes to find the house: eventually Triste pulled up, with the lights off, after positioning the car ready to back into the entrance: he didn't want the trunk to be visible from the road: before he could ring the bell at the gate, the front door opened and an old man walked calmly and confidently up the garden path: he opened the gate into the driveway to the garage as Triste started up the car, putting it into reverse: he backed in slowly, giving the man time to open up the metal door to the garage, which was empty: Triste carried on backing the car till it was inside the garage, a couple of yards from the far wall: at that point he braked and said to Chaves: "OK, out we go": "good evening," the owner of the house greeted them: "good evening," the visitors chimed in unison: Triste opened up the trunk and indicated its contents to Chaves: "you take that end and I'll take this": the body was heavy and they were unable to lower it gently to the ground: it landed with a curious squelch of thick plastic and of liquids squirting into its black interior: "this time tomorrow it'll be in a coffin: you're to come and pick it up with a different vehicle: I'll tell you where you're to take it and where you're to bury it": "see you tomorrow then," Triste cut the brief conversation short twenty-four hours later they were back, loading the rough wooden coffin with the corpse in it into the back of a van: "Timote, that's the name of the village, Timote: when you get there ask for La Celma ranch": it was a three-hundred mile drive but the vehicle was equipped for the occasion: despite the unsurfaced roads and lack of signposts they made it to Timote in seven hours, with one stop at a roadside bar to down a gin and a couple of coffees: when they reached La Celma a good-looking boy rode out to meet them on a dappled horse: "follow me," he said, without saying hello or introducing himself: there was no need: he led them to an outbuilding which was separate from the ranch itself: it was a kind of gigantic hangar for storing grain and farm machinery, with a doorway big enough to accommodate a lorry, but there was nothing in it: their guide got off his horse and flagged Triste into the empty barn: once he was inside, he pointed to a corner and Cristóbal went over to it without giving it a second thought: there were two raised trap doors with some steps leading down to a cellar: "it's to go down there," the young horseman muttered without making the slightest move to help: Triste opened up the van and pulled the rope wound around the coffin to ease it out: when it was over halfway out, he grasped it by the near end: "you take the other end," he said to Chaves: one step at a time, struggling not to stumble under its weight and fall and break his back, Cristóbal edged his way down the thirty-two steps to the cellar, which had an earthen floor: at one end someone had dug a pit: they carried the makeshift coffin over to it and Chaves went up to fetch the rope they'd brought: there was no sign of man or beast: no trace of the youth who had led them there, his horse or any living creature: "we're on our own," he said when he got back down: "never mind, that's nothing new: we've been on our own from the start": they slipped the rope under the coffin, doubled for strength, and lowered it into the earth:

"Chaves," said Triste, "I'll shovel the earth on to the coffin; you're a priest, why don't you say a prayer or something for the man?": "sure," said Chaves, and started to mumble what were presumably the funeral rites: when he came to an end, Triste filled in the hole, climbed the steps, waited for his companion to do the same, shut the trap doors and went straight back to the driver's seat: there was no one in sight as they left the ranch, nor as they drove to the village, which they passed through without stopping: the drive back to the capital, in the daylight this time and with just one stop, took them only six and a half hours: they took the van back to where they'd got it from and hailed a cab to the centre, to find a restaurant that stayed open all afternoon: Triste bought the day's papers, in which the general's kidnap was still headline news, and flicked through them over lunch: they were having a coffee when Triste spoke: "Chaves, you know who we took for a ride to the country?": "yes, Triste: Aramburu: did you have something against him?": "why should I have anything against him?": "because you're a Peronist supporter": "no, Padre, not me: my mother supported the Peronists, that's why I don't like people criticizing them; but I'm not a Peronist supporter: I don't support anybody: and know what? I don't think you do either, I don't think you support anybody any more, am I right, Chaves?": "yes, you're quite right, Triste": when they left the restaurant they went their separate ways: Triste went home and slept for fourteen hours

Chapter 17. Another Storming
of Another Bastille

And cargoes horses
Labourers carnivals fields
The vast world encompassed
By a bird's free flight
ENRIQUE MOLINA, *High Life*

on the 25th May no less, national independence day and the day a new president took office but not power - "Cámpora to govern, Perón to rule" the campaign slogan had run - the president voted in by a largely Peronist electoral majority found himself obliged, in what was virtually his inaugural act, to declare the much-vaunted, oft-proclaimed, eagerly-awaited general amnesty - "give us an amnesty, General; General, give us a general amnesty" - that had become a foregone conclusion: it was a choice between the dentist in the Casa Rosada giving way or the people, in this case a by no means abstract entity, getting their way: in practice, the two options boiled down to much the same thing, or were two sides of the same coin: Cámpora gave way since the people were getting their way, imagining that their heart's desire had been conceded even if the concession existed only in their heart's desire: the people took to the streets at the crack of dawn, demanding and claiming what they had been promised, ready to go on chanting till their prisoners were handed over, ready to get them back by whatever means were available: thousands of citizens pouring into the streets celebrating what they had still, in the course of that day, to snatch from the jailor's clutches

no order was responsible for the convergence of that multitude on Villa Devoto Jail, whose walls had witnessed one of the more eventful moments of Triste's by all accounts eventful life: no radio or television broadcast hinted at the desirability of such a move: no political rallies sowed the seeds of that unanimous decision to descend - "in a tide of seething fury" - on Calle Bermúdez, clamouring outside its infamous walls for the release of all political prisoners: but by mid-afternoon they were there in their thousands: exhausted from the revelries that had been going on since early morning, sweating, shouting, driven by a force unparalleled in the nation's previous, or subsequent, history: the words of their cacophonous chant were surprisingly clear: we want the prisoners released right now: if not we'll storm the gates and get them out, no matter what the consequences: the prison governor could not help but get the message, nor could the guards who from their posts had kept their machine guns trained on the crowd all day, nor the prisoners who were as keen to get out as the crowd was to get them out: whether through intuition, insight or basic common sense - always a sound political guide - everyone outside the gates knew that if they failed to get what they wanted that day, they would never get it: those inside the jail had reached that same conclusion, that same conviction long before: the 25th of May or never: that afternoon the police realized too: it doesn't matter - except perhaps to meticulous recorders of historical detail, who will never be capable of interpreting any event involving more than two or three individuals - and it didn't matter to those on either side of the wall that afternoon, whether or not a telephone conversation took place with President Cámpora - a conversation whose function could only be to pass the buck for opening the prison doors from the prison warders to the top of the ladder: on the President's orders, on the President's head - what mattered was that the prisoners should be released, that for whatever reason the people's demands should finally be met, a meagre reward for twenty years of unalleviated frustrations, but a reward nonetheless: there were no negotiations as such, but the crowd's irate chanting and the warders' enforced silence set up a dialogue whose meaning was clear to all with ears to hear: the first prisoners were released in dribs and drabs, like sops thrown to a beggar in the covert hope of making him forget the banquet: but, after the first few releases, there was not a chance in hell of staying the turbulent flood that left the prison drained: Cámpora had kept his word, had acted - or let others act - as befitted not a man in office but a man in power: but he was not in power: Perón held power, he only held office: no matter how strong the pressures put on him, the granting of an amnesty was an act of power that a man who had occupied the highest seat of office in another's name could perform only at risk of what the all-powerful Perón himself liked to call "pulling the plug out": the arrangements for the return from exile, for the "definitive return home of General Perón", were irrevocably speeded up: "I have to go back because Cámpora let the rabble out," Perón would insist to his doctor, when the latter advised against his leaving Spain: the 25th May 1973 did not represent a lack of power, a weakening of power, a withholding of power or an erosion of power: it was more of an own-goal scored by the agent of power: but between the goalposts of power there are countless goalkeepers behind the goalkeeper who is seen to the crowd, and the ball never hits the back of the net: Cámpora would spend the rest of his life, finally dying wretchedly in exile, expiating that blunder and two or three more he mercifully made before being forced to resign

among the countless goalkeepers behind the goalkeeper seen to the crowd - names of individuals and parties are of little consequence - were Major Mendoza's bosses: they took their precautions with, on more than one occasion, notable success: as far as the events that took place in and around Villa Devoto Jail were concerned, it has to be said that they showed considerable political acumen, and knew exactly what needed to be done to serve their interests the start of the 25th May saw Triste in La Libertad bar in Calle Bermúdez, exactly opposite the main prison gates: for those released after serving their sentences, the bar's name acts as a sort of reminder of their new state: but La Libertad is more than just a bar facing the prison gates: it is more of a prison outpost: if you have a relative inside and take him a little something on visitors' day - cigarettes perhaps, or oranges, bread or jam - the warders in charge of checking the parcels will find some way of rendering the present unusable - if you happen to have taken a pack of cigarettes, for example, they'll take a sturdy awl out of their tool kit and spike the carton in three or four different places, crosswise and lengthwise, making sure the awl goes right through and comes out the other side: with holes in them, half the cigarettes will be unsmokable - but if you buy what you want to take your relative in La Libertad, where everything from tobacco to oranges can be procured at an exorbitant price, often two or three times more than its market value, you can be sure your gift will reach its destination intact: no one will break anything open to see if there's a file or pistol hidden inside: the product will have been checked by the owner of La Libertad, who gives his business partners - the warders who turn a blind eye; all the warders, in other words - a cut of the profits: that morning Triste propped himself up against the bar in La Libertad to order a gin and suss out what was going on: the bar's clients were, not surprisingly, police officers, not released prisoners: the latter want to get away from the place as fast as they can, and stop off for a drink only when they're safely out of the district: they're not going to risk being sent back to the place they've just left, or which has just abandoned them to their fate, by some tetchy prison warder in civvies: Triste's observations were cut short by the appearance in the doorway of Chaves and another individual whom Triste had seen before on other compromising assignations: the three of them were to hang around the area for the whole day, so it was best to get on a good footing from the start, to avoid unnecessary friction: Duarte - the surname by which he was known to Chaves and Cristóbal - went to the far end of the bar and talked to the owner, who was obviously in his confidence: at that stage some agreement must have been reached over the use of certain facilities required by subsequent events: regular use of the phone, the right to take refuge in the bar should the expected disturbances make it necessary to close, access to a special vantage-point if the shutters had to be pulled down over the doors and windows: all of which had its price, and Duarte had no more qualms about handing over the money before the bemused eyes of the clientele than did the bar's owner about publicly admitting to accepting bribes: a not inconsiderable amount of pesos changed hands: immediately after, Duarte went to use the phone, which he would continue to do once an hour till late afternoon, when the gathering crowd made any update unnecessary because the action was taking place in front of their eyes

after three hours had gone by, Triste, who had so far kept his mouth shut, asked: "apart from waiting for something or other to happen, just what are we meant to be doing in this place?": "watching, remembering," was Duarte's terse reply: "watching what? remembering what?" Triste demanded clarification: "faces, young man, faces," Duarte specified tartly: "prisoners' faces, demonstrators' faces, or policemen's faces?": "this is no time for jokes, we're in the thick of something big: I don't know exactly what the mechanism is going to be, but today a whole lot of guys are going to come out of those gates opposite who ought not to be coming out: since we can't put them back inside just yet, we'll have to find a way of keeping tabs on them": "or eliminating them, you mean," Cristóbal ventured: "or eliminating them," Duarte confirmed; "there's going to be hundreds of them coming out, thousands even … God knows how many, they're going to let the whole lot out: I'm familiar with more than one of their faces: there are other observers like us planted in all the surrounding streets and they're familiar with more than one face too: I'm going to point out ten faces to the two of you, just ten, don't worry: I want you both to take a good look at them and fix those faces firmly in your heads: tonight we'll look at some photos and jog our memories: you've got to be able to remember them no matter when or where, even if they change the way they look, even if they grow a beard, a moustache, dye their hair, wear dark glasses: today we know where they are, in a week's time we may not": "you mean they'll have gone underground?" Triste asked: "yes, if they get that far," Duarte clarified: "you want to eliminate them first?": "now look, since you've asked me a straight question, I'll give you a straight answer: yes, this is the start of a mopping-up operation designed to weed out the most dangerous ones at least, in the course of the coming week: any objections?": "objections to what?": "to taking care of the guys I'm going to point out to you?": "ten of them?": "ten of them": "it can be done"

they didn't stay in La Libertad: Duarte kept making phone calls and co-ordinating their activities: the crowd's movements allowed them to go some six hundred yards down the road to have lunch in a decent restaurant: at four o'clock they learnt that various columns of demonstrators of varying political denominations were making for the threatening metal gates in Calle Bermúdez: at five they saw the first demonstrators arrive and take up position: at six it looked as though everyone who might be coming had got there, but Duarte was certain more were on the way: the prisoners, including some common offenders, were released before all those wanting to take part in the drama were able to make it to the tacitly agreed rendezvous: there were many who had hoped to be there and fortunately arrived too late "that one over there," said Duarte, pointing to a man stepping out on to the pavement: Triste looked at the man, looked at him long and hard to engrave him on his mind forever, even after he was dead: "that one," Duarte repeated, and Triste looked, his mind blank, all his energies devoted to taking in the image: La Libertad had closed and they had opted to stay out in the street, near the bar door, mingling with the crowd, waiting like everyone else, looking like everyone else at the faces of the prisoners coming out, except that most people were looking for just one special face, a face loved, respected or simply needed: "that one," Duarte said again, and Triste looked, wondering vaguely how many other people there were looking for the same reasons: Duarte kept moving off, disappearing into the crowd and coming back with instructions: the three of them - he, Chaves and Triste - didn't look as though they were together: that was what saved the priest and Cristóbal: a voice a few yards behind Triste suddenly rang out: "bloody jailor," and the voice's owner pointed an accusing finger at Duarte: "he's a cop: I've seen him inside, he's a plant", and Triste looked on as eight, ten, fifty men hurled themselves on Duarte and started to beat him up: mindful of what had happened to Héctor, Triste edged away, took Chaves by the arm and dragged him off in the opposite direction: "come on," he said: "but...," Chaves tried to interject: "let them kill the bastard: we're getting out of this, Chaves"

they saw no more of Duarte, but next day someone slipped under Triste's door an envelope with eight photographs in it, each with a slip listing the individual's personal details: also enclosed was a note that said: "deal with the ones you recognize; return the photos and slips for the others; two million a head": "sixteen million," Triste totted up and dialled a number: "can I speak to Father Chaves, please?" he asked, almost fondly: "speaking," the priest's voice at the other end of the line: "four o'clock in the Tortoni, Padre: there's sixteen million at stake": "thank you for ringing, my son: you can count on me," Chaves feigned for whoever he was with: "I'm counting all right," said Triste and put the phone down

Chaves had long ago ceased to be the man in the trenchcoat: he now wore the staid clothes expected of a man of his calling, but with a classy cut: he was making his pile too, and felt entitled to some little luxuries: that afternoon he came into the café beaming: as he ordered his whisky, Triste gaped at him: something important had obviously happened: "care to tell me what's up with you, Padre?": "Padre no more: I've quit": "you've quit...?": "quit the cloth: it's all over": "that's something to drink to, Chaves: now we can even be friends: so you had the guts to do it: let's start by being partners, Chaves: how about that for a start?": "haven't we been partners for some time?": "no: we've worked together for some time, but we've not been partners: you had another life, were into things I knew nothing about, I had to fend for myself because you couldn't stick your neck out ... I don't know ... a whole load of crap like that: now we can be partners": they spent a couple of hours in idle conversation, making plans for Chaves' new life, going over things of the past: "and what was all that on the phone about sixteen million?": Triste briefly put him in the picture and showed him the envelope: "we'll go over the photos at home later, when there's no one looking": "and then...?": "we're to liquidate the lot of them": "when do we start?": "tomorrow, Chaves: first thing tomorrow morning"

at six a.m. he took the car out of the garage rented in his name: it wasn't stolen: he'd bought it on hire purchase, it was his, but right now it had different number plates on : it came in handy for work and was less risky than a stolen car: he picked Chaves up at Avenida de Mayo and Salta, and they headed slowly for Barrio Norte: in Calle Vicente López, just off Callao, Triste pulled in at the head of a row of cars that had been parked there overnight: he got out, opened the trunk and took out the same two bags with the machine guns: he got back into the driver's seat with them: they opened the bags and, before tossing them empty on to the back seat, carefully deposited the weapons on the floor by their feet: at seven, the first caretakers to the neighbouring apartment blocks started to come out on to the street: "he's an early bird, Chaves, be ready for him," Triste warned: at twenty past seven, he pointed to a boy coming out of a doorway, the second in the next block: he'd kept the engine ticking over, and said "that one" as they coasted towards him: the boy looked about twenty-five - Triste knew he was precisely twenty-seven - and was on his guard: but by the time he realized what was about to happen, the car was on top of him: when he got alongside, Triste slowed down to allow Chaves to fire: two blasts lifted the young man into the air for a few seconds: as he started to fall, spurts of blood came gushing out of the holes: Triste pulled the handbrake on, leapt out into the roadway cocking a pistol and went over to his side as, before his eyes, he doubled up, contracted, sank to the pavement in search of firm ground: a foot away from his target, he fired just once: a round, black hole in his right temple: with a couple of bounds Triste was back at the wheel, put the .38 on the seat beside him and roared off: people were rushing over to the inexplicable body

they made straight for the garage without putting away their weapons, piled under Chaves' feet: Triste opened up the door and drove in: he carefully locked the door from the inside, got out the machine guns and bags, and placed them in a kind of bunker containing two identical weapons in identical bags: he'd come back in the evening to clean them and get them in perfect working order: he'd leave them there just for the time being: the pistol he left in his toolbench drawer: "let's go, Chaves": only then did the latter get out of the car to leave the garage: Triste double-locked the door before leaving: they went into a bar chosen at random and ordered a couple of coffees and gins: "feeling OK?" Triste asked his partner: "sure, fine ... it's just that ... it's always you that takes care of it: it's the first time I've mowed somebody down like that ...": "in cold blood, you mean? look: I used to think I couldn't do it, that I could only do it if I looked the guy in the eye, if he knew I was about to do him in, but that's all water under the bridge: now I don't give a damn what happens to the bugger: all I care about is making sure he's cold and can't grass on us: I don't give a damn about anything else": Chaves listened attentively, trying vainly to feel the same way: "I'll get used to it," he finally said: Cristóbal smiled at him

Triste went back to his apartment after lunch, at two: someone had slipped under the door, one at a time or in little piles, two hundred notes of ten thousand pesos each: they were scattered all over the floor: he bent down and picked them up, piling them on the kitchen table: there he divided them into separate piles, ordered them, counted them and stacked them in two piles of a million each: finally he put them in two thick brown envelopes: "thanks," he said to no one in particular, thinking of no one in particular: he went to the phone and dialled Chaves' number: he was still living in the apartment attached to the church till he'd fixed himself a place to live, and came straight to the phone: "Chaves," said Triste: "speaking, what's up?" his partner's voice was tinged with alarm: "tell me, Chaves: did you think of saying a prayer as you pressed the trigger?": "yes, I did": "and?": "I couldn't: but I did later, when you got out to finish him off: I prayed for me and for him: and above all I prayed for you, Triste"

Chapter 18. The Underdogs Stay Under

You can't imagine,
my dancing child,
how the taste of mourning
sours the earth
where my heart smoulders.
OTTO RENÉ CASTILLO, *Taste of Mourning*

because Cámpora, despite his lack of power, had "let the rabble out", as Perón put it to his doctor, the date of the general's return - the "definitive return home of our General" - was brought forward: his arrival at Ezeiza International Airport was set for the 20th June 1973, exactly one year ten days before his death: he kept to the announced date, but his plane never touched down at the place where millions - literally - of cheering supporters were waiting to welcome him: instead he landed at Morón military airbase, delivering a bloody historical rebuff to those for whom that moment represented the fulfilment of their most cherished dreams: nonetheless, till the actual moment of his touch-down elsewhere, everything went ahead at Ezeiza and for miles around as if the official welcome were going ahead: the platform from which he was to deliver his speech went up, purveyors of sundry refreshments and souvenirs - photos, national flags, Peronist badges - set about plying their trade, the crowds started to jostle for a place in the huge, milling throng gathered round the central point from which, they had been led to believe, Perón would address them

they came in their millions, from all corners of the republic, in a virtual re-take of the operation mounted at the time of the never-ending exequies for the general's late wife, Eva Duarte, to which Triste had been taken by his mother in its earliest hours: on this occasion too, hundreds of thousands of free tickets were dished out to allow every province to send representatives to the capital, to acclaim the long-awaited messiah on his triumphal entry into the city: hundreds of thousands of free rail or bus tickets, thousands of lorries crammed to bursting point, thousands of private cars: millions of men, women and children, a not inconsiderable proportion of whom had their trips financed as far as the appropriate railway terminus, from where they set off on foot - one, two or even three days before the appointed date - to make sure of being at least in the vicinity of the spot on which their hopes had been trained for so many turbulent years: the posters read: "I shall return a million strong, Evita" printed beneath or beside a picture of the woman Triste remembered as a white doll laid out in her coffin, only her face visible beneath the oval glass panel displaying the holy relic to the visitors' fervour: the posters read: "Perón, Evita, for Socialist Argentina" (which cynics deliberately misread as "Perón, Evita, forget Socialist Argentina", for that is what their contribution to their long-suffering nation's tortuous history had effectively meant): as before, Triste looked at the sea of faces, now weary, marked with the indelible signs of malnutrition, but happy to have come from the most far-flung corners of that unknown hinterland, not this time to bid farewell to the "champion of the poor" but to welcome the widowed saviour joined in matrimony anew - for the third time, in fact - to a dancer prone to bouts of hysteria and forced on to the political stage, the long-awaited widower of the fair, beloved First Lady, about to land trailing in his wake a secretary-cum-factotum, José López Rega, about whom nothing was known except that he enjoyed a privileged position among the general's retainers, fulfilling the supplementary functions of gardener and astrologist: as before, Triste looked at the sea of faces, now changed even if, as before, they belonged to individuals who would take advantage of the specially laid on transport never again to return to their villages of origin, setting themselves up in makeshift shacks, swelling the already proliferating ring of shanty towns surrounding Buenos Aires, with fewer hopes and fewer dreams than their predecessors twenty years before, but with the added inducement of the prodigal general whose return merited the killing of the fatted calf: as before, Triste looked at the sea of faces, now changed also because he was looking at them from a different angle

no more Rosario Artola's son, dead and buried those who had peopled his brief, harsh childhood, a never-ending winter suddenly ended by the eclipse of his mother's meagre existence; no more the tentative adolescent who had tried his luck at billiards and paid for his effrontery with the irreversible loss of his touch, the impeccable co-ordination of hand and eye that had been a hallmark of his early youth; no more the believer in certain principles whose existence had been nipped in the bud in the course of his first encounters with Chaves; no more the sentimental youth who twice in one day had braved the shelling of the Plaza de Mayo simply because of an obscure intuition that had kept him there to witness, not the massacre, but an individual tragedy that mattered to him alone; no more the multiple selves he had been and ceased to be in successive changes of skin, each one thicker than the last, Triste went with Chaves to Ezeiza Airport to join a group of armed bodyguards hired to protect against possible attack the area round the presidential platform where Perón was to deliver yet another dazzling speech: "comrades..." he would begin, letting three, four, five minutes elapse before repeating the magic watchword that never failed to unleash an outburst of chanting and shouting that would inevitably give way to the insistent drumbeats and all-too-familiar strains of the official march *Perón's Young Heroes*, epitomizing the wayward musical tastes of the newly restored regime's official composers: Triste and Chaves, pistols in their belts, in the former case flick-knife at the ready, sought out and located a man called Maidana, the boss of some organization whose name ended with "order", deliberately mumbled to conceal the fact that it had no official status: "Comrade" Maidana: "good morning, comrades," came Comrade Maidana's greeting: "morning," Triste replied curtly on their joint behalf: "over there, comrades," he ordered: they would see him only once more, briefly, in the course of that afternoon: and they took up their position by one of the side supports to the wooden platform: "what the hell do they want an armed guard here for?" Triste wondered out loud, not expecting his partner to reply: if anyone goes berserk here, he thought, the crowd will lynch him, and the image of Duarte and Héctor came back into his mind: apart from which the security cordon of which they appeared to be a part was only one of possibly hundreds disposed at various strategic points, each one corresponding to some different Peronist faction

supporters of the corporate state, loyal devotees of the general in life and if necessary in death (it would be necessary), scores of Peronist youth movements, the Peronist Student Youth Movement, the Peronist Workers' Youth Movement, the plain Peronist Youth Movement, the Women's Branch of the Peronist Movement, the Revolutionary Armed Forces and the Montoneros joined in a sudden effusion of brotherly solidarity that would set them both on the slippery slope to disaster, the General Workers' Confederation, the 62 Organizations Standing at Perón's Side, and a whole range of outlandish labels and banners, enough to make any political scientist despair, each label and each banner with its own bodyguards or security corps, or - in cases where numbers were insufficient to warrant a division of labour into slogan-shouters and guardians against real or imaginary attack by the oligarchy - with every single member of the group armed and at the ready: what the hell are we doing here, Triste wondered again and again as his careful scrutiny of the human vista before his eyes revealed the existence of more and more security patrols: only later that day did he realize why he had been given such orders, why he had been posted at that point

it was many hours later, some time after the first rumours that Perón was not going to turn up, that his plane was circling overhead uncertain whether to land, that it had finally been decided that he would touch down at the military compound at Morón, that the General's advisers had opposed his landing at Ezeiza because of the risks involved in exposing himself to his supporters, whose sheer numbers made it all too likely that some deranged assassin might be lurking in the crowd ready to cut down the supreme symbol of national unity: it was some time after, when - as Triste remarked, pondered, saw - the faces of those present began to register disappointment, dismay, disenchantment with their leader's behaviour, which would nonetheless be justified by appeal to the conspiracy theory according to which Perón was a great man but surrounded by enemies of the people, to which one might have replied, had anyone been prepared to listen, that he couldn't be such a great man if he was such a bad judge of those around him; it was at the moment when the thousands or tens of thousands of transistor radios began to inform those who had made the endless journey by train or bus, those who had trekked for miles and miles on foot, those who packed in the backs of rickety trucks had come from the northern jungles or frozen southern wastes, that General Perón had indeed landed at Morón and had let his millions of supporters down: it was - as Triste was quick to recognize - just after the news had spread round the crowd, in that second's gap separating the fruitless wait from the decision to disperse and go home, that the first shot was fired: Triste heard someone giving orders in a peremptory military tone but he couldn't make out what the orders were - Chaves would later clarify that the first orders had been given in French, to mercenaries of the former OAS who had fought in Algeria under General Raoul Salam: after ten, twenty seconds had elapsed, the orders came in clearly Argentine Spanish, addressed to the bodyguards posted round the platform: for it was from the platform that shots had been fired at the crowd, and Triste realized that was why they had been stationed there and he looked round at the people and at Chaves, who was equally disconcerted but was aiming his pistol ready to shoot: "hold it, Chaves," Triste shouted just in time to stop him joining in the massacre: he rushed over to him and seized him by the arm: his partner stared at him, letting him take the initiative: Triste grabbed hold of him and dived with him under the platform, pushing him on all fours to the back: Chaves understood without Triste having to say a word: "what the hell do you think you were about to do, Chaves?": "something awful": "exactly, that's what you were about to do: something awful: just as well I stopped you: they're human beings like you and me, people who believe in something when we stopped believing long ago: they support Perón: we support no one: so we're not going to kill them for that, are we?": "of course not": they had flung themselves to the ground under the platform, with their guns trained on the crowd in case anyone had his eyes on them: a man came up behind them, pointing a machine gun at them: Triste said nothing but waved him over, his pistol clearly visible in his raised hand: when the man got to his side and squatted down, laying his machine gun on his thighs to light a cigarette and hear what Triste had to say, the latter swung round, lowering his arm, and fired twice: the man was blasted backwards, his face a bleeding mass: Triste took the machine gun which had fallen to the ground and signalled to Chaves to try to sneak out from under the back of the platform: as hoped, they emerged to find themselves behind the hired assassins, amid a welter of orders and counter-orders: Triste spotted a jeep some five hundred yards away and decided to make for it: they ran flat out, not stopping to look behind them, till they reached it: Triste handed the machine gun to Chaves before climbing into the driver's seat and fiddling with the dashboard: he had got the engine running when he looked up and saw the boy racing towards them, pistol at the ready: Chaves, still standing on the tarmac, cut him short with two rounds of fire: he leapt in as the jeep made off: Triste put his foot flat down on the accelerator, and they drove across country till soon the platform, the crowd, the firing were left behind them in the distance: they could hear the far-off, muffled noise of screaming: they were approaching a badly lit road streaming with people slowly making their way back, presumably, to the capital: "let's dump the jeep and machine gun here, and join them: we'll end up somewhere, whatever happens": "good idea, yes, let's join them": it was the first time Chaves had expressed an interest in other people: or a fear of being alone

Chapter 19. The Tank

the constant, obsessive repetition of the final scenario inflicted by him on so many victims accustomed Triste to the eyes of the dying, of the dead: accustomed him to the idea, which he recognized as a limitation, that those startled, terrified, pleading, craving or just blank eyes marked a boundary beyond which he would never be able to go

both Triste and Chaves were hard-bitten men of action, with the right credentials to qualify them for admission to the groups that from 1973 onwards would hijack the nation, its destiny, its dreams, under the successive names of the AAA, the Strategic Command and finally the "Joint Forces", the latter representing the fusion and culmination of the entire security network of a state governed by the notion of the "internal enemy", where - as Rodolfo Walsh stated in print at the time - the AAA were the three branches of the Armed Forces: Army, Navy and Air Force working in unison to put an end to his precarious existence as outspoken journalist and bereaved father: effectively, some time after the episode at Ezeiza, thanks to the fact that Triste and his partner's superiors in the hierarchy of corruption never found out about their last-minute desertion, partly because the few eye-witness accounts were so confused, partly also because Maidana had been killed in the thick of the events he had helped to precipitate, the two men were invited on an outing: it was shortly after Perón's comeback, the day an unknown voice over the phone informed Triste of the need to be ready to be picked up that afternoon with Chaves, in one of the vast underground car parks beneath Avenida 9 de Julio, by a car whose driver would recognize them: Triste could drive there and leave his car in the car park: after they had completed whatever the organisers of the outing had in mind, the same chauffeur would drive them back to the car park: Cristóbal wondered if it could be a trap - there were plenty of people in Buenos Aires ready to wreak revenge on him and Chaves, should they be recognized - but it was all too complicated: anyone bent on revenge would gun them down in the street or ambush them at home: he rang his partner, who had received similar instructions and wanted them to meet beforehand to discuss the implications of this new, tricky situation

"we've got to go, Chaves, whatever happens": "I know we've got to go: what's more, I thought I recognized the voice on the phone": "and does that help any?": "the opposite, Triste, if anything: I'm pretty sure it was Captain Rojas Agüero, from naval intelligence: he's a specialist in torture, the use of electric shocks, that sort of thing": "what exactly are you getting at?": "I'm very much afraid, Triste, that they're going to propose an extension of our sphere of activity, in return for more cash, of course": "an extension? how can we do more than kill people?": "not more, Triste, less: hell comes before death, not after": "I get you; it's not my scene": "but they can force you to do it": "no, Chaves, they can't force us to do it: they can't force you to do it either"

at half past four sharp, Triste swerved into the space between two other cars in the vast underground parking lot, and braked: he switched the lights and engine off, offered Chaves a cigarette and settled back to wait: the two men appeared on foot before three minutes were up: "we've got the cars round the other side: would you kindly accompany us?": the formulation betrayed a police officer: "cars?" Triste inquired: "yes, there's two of them: one for each of you": "what for?": "for the same reason that you're going to have to let us frisk you to check you're not armed": "we are armed," said Triste, raising his hands above his head and nodding to Chaves to do the same: "there's no need to put your hands up," said the one calling the tune: "I'd rather avoid the risk of some fatal misunderstanding," Cristóbal replied; "we've got pistols strapped to our chests: take them, please": the one who hadn't opened his mouth, obviously a subaltern, did as he was told: "now you can frisk us: we're unarmed," Triste assured him: the hireling deftly ran his hands over their two bodies, without finding any offensive weapon: he chose to ignore Triste's knife: "so now we're all quite happy, are we? will you kindly tell me what all this is about?" Cristóbal asked: "of course: Captain Rojas Agüero wants you to visit the building we're fitting out: it's not yet working at full capacity, but you can get an idea of what's planned: we're not allowed to say where it is, so you'll each have to travel on the floor of a car, blindfolded, and that's also how you'll be brought back here in a few hours' time: that's all": "OK," said Triste, locking up his own car, "let's go"

they walked to the far end of the parking lot: there they found two other men, one in each car, on the back seat : they politely got out to hold the car doors open for Triste and Chaves, who climbed in and sat down: their guards got straight back inside: each of them took out of their pockets a broad, black cloth band, with long tapes at either end: "I'm going to blindfold you," Triste's guard informed him; "then please lie down on the floor": having accommodated himself on the car floor, Triste asked: "like that?": "that'll do nicely," the guard replied, doing his best to avoid treading on him with his feet: the scene was repeated down to the last detail with Chaves: they finally set off: the journey, according to Cristóbal's calculations, took about thirty-five minutes, which meant not only that they were still in Buenos Aires but that they weren't all that far from their starting-point: whatever the case, when they were given permission to sit up and had their blindfolds taken off, they found themselves in an enclosed space, a kind of covered inner courtyard used as a garage on account of its size: its smooth grey walls had no distinguishing feature other than the lack of distinguishing features: the man who had brought them there left them alone: in what seemed like a full five minutes before their hosts came out to welcome them, they carefully inspected everything in sight, including the two cars in which they had been driven there: they were green Falcons, identical to the ones that later were to become the mobile symbols of an omnipresent government-sponsored terror: at the time nothing they saw gave them any indication of what was to come

Captain Rojas Agüero and Father Balmes emerged together from a side entrance, a different entrance from the one their subordinates had used to enter the building: "how are you, Chaves?" was Rojas Agüero's greeting, followed by "you must be Artola": "yes," Triste responded drily, shaking the naval officer's hand: "Father Chaves, how nice to see you here, though I suppose I shouldn't call you Father Chaves any more, should I?": "indeed, Father; I left the priesthood some time ago: a vocational crisis, as I'm sure you'll appreciate": "quite, quite, but I trust you haven't given up your patriotic convictions together with the cloth?": "oh no, Father Balmes, never"; so the conversation went for the next quarter of an hour: finally Rojas Agüero took charge and explained what it was all about: "you must be wondering, gentlemen, rightly so, why I've had you brought here; indeed: you must be wondering where you are; I'm only too happy to tell you: you're inside what is going to be a detention centre for Marxist subversives, which will be devoted to the prime task of re-education and rehabilitation: we want to take those who fall prisoner in our fight against terrorism and international communism and turn them into instruments for the good of society, for the good of our cause: I have no doubt that, on seeing the admittedly controversial nature of the rehabilitation methods used in our institution, less seasoned men than yourselves might doubt their effectiveness: but I am sure experience has acquainted you with the uses of rigour: rigour to what end, you may ask: I shall tell you: first, to rid the prisoner of his demons: our enemies talk of interrogation: nothing could be further from our intentions: if obtaining information were our concern, we would use purely chemical methods to extract detailed confessions: that's not what we're here for: we plan to make rigorous use of what the layman calls torture - we call it physical treatment - not to extract confessions but to exorcise demons: not torture: exorcism, gentlemen: Father Balmes will support me: now you know where we are, I shall answer your other question: we've had you brought here to take a look round the place, tour its installations, where possible see them at work, and have a little think as to whether you'd like to join us and contribute to our good work"

when he got to the end of his long sermon, uttered with conviction and - Triste thought - vindictive relish, the naval officer and the priest called Balmes asked Chaves and Cristóbal with the utmost courtesy to accompany them on an inspection tour: first, Rojas Agüero ushered them into his office and offered them a glass of whisky, which they both eagerly accepted and gulped down: "have another," the naval officer encouraged: "why not?" said Chaves: the second glass of whisky made the four men more relaxed and facilitated the following stage: they went into a preliminary chamber, which in some ways reminded Cristóbal of the cell where he had first been detained in the police station out at Berisso: here, as there, the dominant note was concrete, concrete floors, concrete walls, concrete ceiling, and here too there was a wide gutter for the prisoners to relieve themselves: but there was something here that had not existed in that old provincial common cell: rings fixed round the walls, at intervals of approximately a foot and a half: to chain people to, Triste thought: they all inspected the room as if going round a third-rate museum or a house for sale, but no one said a word: what needed saying was all too obvious: before they left, Chaves looked up at the ceiling and noticed the lighting: anaemic light bulbs hanging some four yards from the ground, protected by thick, round metal grilles as if in a squash court: there were no windows: from that oppressive area they went into what looked like an operating theatre, tiled from floor to ceiling, with two white metal tables with grooves on either side, like those used in morgues to carry out autopsies: the blood that would flow into those grooves would belong to living beings: the operating tables had straps riveted on to their sides, to hold the victims down: Rojas Agüero noticed Triste looking intently at a coil of wires with threatening metal terminals, manipulated by an insulated prod, and hastened to put the record straight: "that's for electric torture, Señor Artola: like to have a go?": "perhaps some other time, when there's someone to try on, don't you think?": "that's easily arranged: we can fetch someone from elsewhere in the building: there's no shortage of prisoners: what we need is people trained to treat them": "not today, Captain," Triste demurred, "another time: no need to bother": "as you wish," the naval officer acquiesced: they went into a courtyard: the stench and the spectacle suddenly confronting them took them aback: two hefty men were holding down a third puny-looking man, naked, his body covered in bruises and weals of every conceivable shape and size, grasping him by the hair and plunging his head into a tank brimming over with filthy water, urine and excrement: ten, twenty seconds went by, the victim went on writhing and they let him raise his mouth and nose above water level: at that point the man vomited up part of what he had been forced to swallow, part of what had started to reach his lungs: he kept on vomiting and spluttering and whimpering: Triste had to fight back a violent retch: the two others plunged the man's head back into the excrement: "this is the tank," Rojas Agüero explained, "a treatment with a very high success rate, leading the individual concerned to vomit up words, names and demons": "an exorcism," Balmes ratified: ten, twenty, thirty seconds were taken up by these explanations: "how's it going?" Rojas Agüero asked the torturers: "a toughie: won't let out a thing," they replied: another ten seconds went by: the man had stopped writhing and resisting: "don't worry, just carry on, lads," the naval officer instructed: "but of course," they reassured him: ten more seconds: "I think he's given up on you, gentlemen," Triste ventured: they hastily lifted the prisoner's head out of the tank: they let him fall to the floor: from out of his body gushed a thick spurt of excrement: again Triste had to suppress a violent desire to retch as he stood there, pale, stiff and sad: total silence and terror on Chaves' part: one of the torturers bent down over the victim and prised open his eyelids: "not yet, but he's not far off: couldn't take it, must have had some internal rupture: give him your blessing, Father Balmes": "as you wish, my son," and he started to chant in Latin as he went over to the body on the ground: the nearer he got, the faster the Latin and the greater the expression of loathing on the priest's face: till he reached him and poked him with his foot: "dead," he said, and started to lay into the body with his sturdy shoes, all the while screeching: "I commend your spirit, filthy Marxist, you can go to heaven if you deserve it, but not with my blessing, and if not you can go to hell," followed by more kicks till the flesh gave way and all the liquids separated by nature flooded into a single cavity and the body went on receiving kicks that rained harder and harder till it slurped as though it were full of thick soup: Triste couldn't contain himself any longer and threw up, went on throwing up, he couldn't stop retching just as the priest couldn't stop shrieking: "you'll go to hell, and do you know what hell is like, you bastard?": another kick: "a sea of shit like you've just swallowed": another kick: "a sea of shit for all eternity": yet another kick: "but what do you know about hell," calming down a bit, no longer lashing out at the morass of fluids spilling on to the ground at his feet: "when you probably don't even know who St. Bonaventure was, you poor bastard: a sea of shit for all eternity": Triste had stopped throwing up: sweating, fists clenched, the priest came back to join Rojas Agüero, Chaves and Cristóbal, his audience, for the other two didn't count, they'd seen all there was to see, done all there was to do

Triste having just about recovered, the four of them went back to the first yard in silence: as they passed the naval officer's office, Triste asked: "if you please, Captain, I think I need another whisky": "come in, pour yourself a glass," Rojas Agüero was as polite as ever: "you seem not to be used to certain things": "no, I'm used to firearms: instant death, practically painless": "but we don't want to kill anyone here: just rehabilitate them": "sure, sure": they were waiting for them in the green Falcons: they blindfolded them, and settled them on the floor: in just over half an hour's time they were back at their original point of departure: "what did Rojas say as we were taking our leave?" Chaves asked, ashen-faced and shaking: "that we were to think it over carefully": "and what are you thinking?": "that this isn't for us, Chaves: did you see that dead man's eyes? his eyes were different: shooting is cleaner: though maybe when it comes to it we're just as bad": "no, Triste: we haven't sunk as low as that": "then pack your bags, Chaves, we're going to have to make ourselves scarce: they won't let us off the hook just like that": now it was Chaves' turn: he vomited up his fear, his disgust, his conscience: he left it all behind in the underground car park:

they went to find Triste's car and drove off at top speed

they went their separate ways after downing a few drinks, but there was something else Triste had to do before going home to bed: he made his way to Simón Castro's café and hailed his friend: "Simón, what's the most expensive drink you've got in this joint?": "French champagne": "break it out: this one's on me": "celebrating something?": "not exactly: you may not see me around for a while and I want to say goodbye in style": "wherever you're going," Castro said as he pulled out the cork and filled two glasses, "good luck to you, Triste": "thanks, Simón, I think I'm going to need it"

Chapter 20. Triste Thought of Leaving Too

Tomorrow when we are dead may heaven help us
perhaps we shall still have to go on moving
from place to place
RAUL GONZALEZ TUÑON, *Traveller's Tale*

and who, looking at that open river, did not think of a desperate escape across its waters to the source of their dreams? like everyone else, Cristóbal Artola pinned his hopes of a solution on the previously undreamt-of world that existed on its unseen, distant shore: it didn't matter how long it took to get things organized, there were still places left where Major Mendoza, Captain Rojas Agüero and Father Balmes would never be able to reach them: in the terrible years of the 1970s Europe ceased to be the mecca of the intelligentsia and became an obsession for ordinary citizens: people who had never once bothered to make the trip to Bahía Blanca to see the sea began to set their sights on Paris, Madrid or Berlin as places where they might have a better chance of survival than in Buenos Aires

the episode in Rojas Agüero's rehabilitation centre plunged Triste into a period of grim reflection: he would walk round and round the streets, stopping off to slake his gloomy, broody silence at the more prestigious bars on route: he did not go back to Simón Castro's café: with their last drink together, as he was well aware at the time, they had said goodbye for good: he was about to leave the path others had till now carved out for him and go it on his own, free from the dictates of military and other fanatics - he might even take a job - which would make him a prime target: he couldn't allow Simón, his old friend, to get caught up in the net meant for him: if Chaves wanted to come with him, fine: but Triste wasn't going to force his hand: it was quite possible, he thought, that his partner wanted to see how things went for him in hell: he wouldn't try to dissuade him: after a week and a half he rang him and arranged to meet, as in what were now starting to feel like old times, at the Tortoni

"Chaves," he announced, "I'm thinking of going on a journey, a long journey, a one-way journey: any day now: if I stay around here, I know I'll end up a zombie like the guys we saw the other day: a zombie or dead: and all for nothing, because I'm worth nothing, I believe in nothing: if you want to bunk off with me, we can talk about it: if not, forget what I've just said and we won't let it come between us": "no, Triste, I'm not backing out of this one: I want to make a clean break too; things are going from bad to worse and we're the ones who'll get it in the neck; the thing is, I've been thinking it over, trying to work out how to go about it, and I can't come up with any ideas: can you?": "yes: I've got a few": "am I allowed in on them?": "you are": "tell me": and Triste bent forward to whisper to him the results of the previous week's cogitations: "you know as well as I do that we're on their files: they know where we live, they're bound to have our phones tapped - right now they must know we're here, and for all we know one of those dumb-looking guys having a coffee and reading the paper at one of those tables is an informer: they've got access to our bank accounts, they're familiar with our daily routine and they know exactly how much money we've got: since this is a city full of spies, we'll have to leave home and disappear, draw out our money without arousing suspicions, make some money on the side": "and how do we do all that, Triste?": "it's what they, the other lot, call going underground": "the other lot? what other lot?": "our paymasters' enemies: the Montoneros, the ERP": "go underground, Triste?: go into hiding?: but where?": "first of all, one of the shanty towns: a corrugated-iron shack in one of the shanty towns; somewhere where no one knows us, where no one will think of looking for us, because we've got cash and two guys with cash are going to have more sense than to go and sleep on old newspapers in a shanty town: till we've got everything worked out, we stay put where we are": "the devil's advocate would like to know what we do in the meantime if they contact us about a job?": "that all depends, Chaves: if it's relatively straightforward, we do it; if it's too dirty, we speed things up and decamp in a couple of hours flat: leave that to me": "one more thing, Triste: the money we've got, it's not the big-time money you need to go on a long trip, a really long trip": "we'll sort that out later, Chaves: that'll be our last job"

Chaves couldn't stop thinking about that last job Cristóbal had mentioned, about what it meant to go underground, to be wanted men wherever they went, to go it on their own as outlaws: a bright lad, Triste, he reflected, I made a good choice there: he's going to get me out of this, when it was me that messed his life up: without me he'd have ended up as something completely different: a gambler, a pimp, a spiv, all of which would have allowed him to scrape a living in times of war as well as in times of peace: I got him into this mess, and now he's going to get me out of it: if he gets out, that is, he checked himself, if he manages to save his own skin: we'll more than likely go to the wall together: fucked up, kaput, like bloody idiots, caught in our own net: if it weren't for Triste, I'd blow my brains out

they saw each other again the next day, as if they had agreed to meet at the same time and the same place: they couldn't help but go on talking about it, go on mulling it over, there was no need to make arrangements to meet again at the same table twenty-four hours later: a week later they would be somewhat taken aback to discover that their afternoon meeting had become a habit, without either of them having said a word about it: they both avoided the phone like the plague: neither would ring the other to fix a meeting: both of them, without realizing for some time that they had fallen into a common routine, would leave home early in the morning, never after nine, returning only late at night, never before one or two: they would wander the streets, take a taxi to some outlying district and walk at random, going into bars and liquor stores to down a solitary glass and watch a distant game of cards, going back to Avenida de Mayo for a late meal and careful perusal of the papers: Triste had also acquired the habit of following the news in the press, of reading his own story in between the lines of national events, in between the lines of an alternately mounting and falling tension that weighed like a millstone on his hopes: one afternoon Triste said to Chaves, "come on, let's go somewhere else: there's something important I want to talk to you about": without a word they set off for Constitución, making for the garage where Triste kept his car: on the way they stopped to gaze into several shop windows, to check no one was following them: the garage was probably not under surveillance, but to make quite sure they decided on a change: they'd rent another garage, under a false name, and not use the car again except to take it there and leave it locked up till the day it was needed, a legally-registered car that could even get them across the frontier: that day Triste drove straight down to the waterfront: he looked for a place to pull up where the river on one side and the open spaces, free of buildings, on the other would allow him to feel confident that there were no cars or people around watching them or simply there, ready to pounce: they leant on the concrete balustrade, looking down at the muddy waters, ignoring the rats scuttling over the rocks: "that last job of ours, Chaves," Cristóbal ventured: "right, Triste: what kind of job?": "a kidnap": "we've never done one": "but we know how it's done": "we do, indeed; do you have someone in mind?": "of course: that's why we're here": "who?": "his name is Barros Ortiz": "the construction magnate?": "that's the one": "and what made you pick him?": "I happened to find out where he lives: a passing remark overheard in a café in Palermo: I spent two or three days following things up and found out a couple more things: his regular habits, where he keeps his car: right now we'll have to wait: he's on business in the States: when he gets back he'll be ours for the taking": "what about the ransom?": "we'll see: a hundred thousand maybe": "dollars?": "of course: how else are we going to get out of this place?": "quite right, Triste: dollars it is"

the August rains started and still their phones were silent: bit by bit, Chaves and Triste began to withdraw their deposits from the bank and from the surveillance of whoever might be concerned to keep tabs on them: Triste began to get the necessaries together to build a shack in the shanty town by the railway tracks leading into Retiro Station, known as Villa de Comunicaciones for reasons that clearly had nothing to do with the good connections of its inhabitants, mainly immigrants from Bolivia, Paraguay and the northern provinces of Argentina: "we'll have to stash the money away in the shack, Chaves: no one in their right mind will think of looking for it there," Triste announced one day: they took it in turns to go to the shanty town: some nights one or other of them would stay behind to eat, sleep and live out a portion of his life so as not to attract attention with a hasty, unannounced, definitive move: they kept a constant, obsessive look out for possible informers, avoiding those who in all likelihood were not watching their movements: they kept quiet about their plans, the alarming future they had to brave as best they could: they lay low biding their time in an unacknowledged attempt to avoid, in their present state of nerves, making some mistake which in the circumstances could well be fatal just before the end of the month, as spring was beginning to be felt in the air and the lives of Triste and Chaves were proceeding cautiously and uneventfully (with Chaves growing ever more depressed and dependent), their plans suffered a first, dangerous setback: Cristóbal was the first to find out, when he bought the papers at five in the morning on his way home to bed: he decided to go straight to Chaves' apartment, without waiting for their afternoon rendezvous: the latter opened the door still half asleep, in a state of confusion and alarm: "what's up, Triste?": "drink this," said Cristóbal, pouring him a whisky, "and splash some cold water on your face": Chaves did as he was told, and rounded on Triste: "would you care to tell me what the hell is going on?": "Barros Ortiz arrived back from the United States yesterday morning": "I know that: I read it in the evening papers": "but in the morning papers, which I bought just ten minutes ago, there's a sequel": "oh yes? what?": "at half past seven, as Barros Ortiz was getting out of his car to go into his house, he was shot in the back of the head: someone made him put his hands on the car roof, as if to search him for arms, and shot him in the back of the head": Chaves stared down at his feet

Chapter 21. The First War Photographs

The stark military mountains
put their deadly gorges on the alert.
CARLOS PELLICER. *Assembled Figures*

on the 11th September of that bitter year of 1973, Salvador Allende was mowed down in La Moneda Palace, taking with him the heady illusions of all those revolutionaries who had thought power could be won by non-revolutionary means: no one - "no citizen of Buenos Aires, drunk or asleep" - could fool himself any longer about the nature of the road that lay ahead: to arms, by arms alone: Triste immediately realized that his time was running out, that it was now or never if he was to make a break: "Chaves," he announced to his panic-stricken partner, "if we can't have a kidnap, then it'll have to be a hold-up": "and what hold-up victim is going to have all we need in his wallet?": "a foreign currency dealer": "that's not such a bad idea: do you know one?": "yes, I do, but let's sleep on it for the time being: if we go ahead with the plan, we'll have to kill him"

it was then that they contacted him: just Triste: it was the first - and last - time they hadn't contacted Chaves as well: "Chaves has been around too much, his face is known to too many people, he won't do for this job," was the explanation he got from the man who confronted him at the door to his apartment block, at noon on the 12th September: "let's go up to your place, so I can give you the low-down": he was carrying a parcel in his hand: as soon as they got into the apartment he started unwrapping it frantically: Triste expected it to be a bomb, but it was a camera: "ever used

176

one of these?" the man asked him: "never," he lied: Triste
made it his business to know about gadgets of every kind:
"it's dead easy," the visitor pronounced, "you just have to
press here": "where?": "here": "I get it": a minute's
demonstration: "got it? try it yourself": "let's see now,"
Triste hesitated: "right first time, congratulations": "and
what have I got to photograph?" Triste inquired naively:
"you mean who, my dear Artola": "all right, who?": "look,
this is the gist of it: today everyone's going to take to the
streets: Peronists, Communists, Socialists, even the Radicals
are going to be out demonstrating: and of course the
Montoneros and the ERP: they think they can do what they
like in this country, but they also know things are more
complicated than that": "what do you mean, that they can do
what they like?": "that they're sanctioned by the law:
sanctioned by the law, my foot: when the time comes, not
one of them'll be left alive": "of course, we can't have them
taking the law into their own hands," Triste commiserated,
going on to inquire, "have you thought of re-educating them,
rehabilitating them?": "I can see you're on my wavelength:
that's exactly what we'd like: in fact, we're working on it
right now, setting up rehabilitation and re-education centres,
as you so rightly put it: but a lot of them won't collaborate;
and they're a cancer, an epidemic, believe you me: the ones
who won't collaborate will have to be exterminated ... well,
that comes after": "after what?": "after today, which is
decisive," said the frustrated rehabilitator: "oh, right ... you
were saying they were going to take to the streets": "yes,
today, the Montoneros and the ERP: but since they're on
their guard, they're not stupid, the leaders will have their
heads covered": "and I've got to take their pictures with
their heads covered? I don't...": "no, no, that's not what I'm
getting at, I'll spell it out to you and you'll see it couldn't be
simpler: first of all, some of them, quite a lot of them, the
ones who are less heavily involved, who are going along as
extras, will have their heads uncovered: you're to photograph

all of them: secondly, they'll have to take a break every now and then, the demonstration is going to stretch for forty or fifty blocks, it'll be the biggest demonstration ever seen in this country: they'll have to walk for miles, and it's starting to get hot: there's bound to be the odd one who's stupid enough, even if he's one of their leaders, to lift his hood up to mop his face: that's what you're to look out for: you can be sure of it: they may know all about weapons, security, guerrilla warfare, but they'll get hot and lift up their hoods": "think so?": "you'll see, you'll see for yourself": "so I ...": "you go and take their picture: here," handing him a press card, with a photo taken from police archives, innocuous, almost anonymous, but enough to identify him: "you'll be safer with this: if anyone says anything to you, you're a journalist": "that's what I always wanted to be": "and wouldn't we like that too, but we can't have everything our way, can we?": "no, of course not ... and afterwards?": "afterwards you're to go home and wait for me to come and pick up the camera": "at what time?": "half past ten sharp"

"Chaves," Cristóbal called out to him in a hoarse whisper: it was three in the afternoon and he'd been waiting for him in a nearby doorway for some time: there was no one around in the siesta-time heat, no prying eye: "come on, I've got to talk to you, follow me": they walked for two hundred yards till a taxi passed: Triste gave the driver the name of a street in Palermo: there they found a café that was still open: "they've asked me to do a job, a dirty job: you've got to help me do it without doing it": "I don't understand": Cristóbal gave him a brief report of his encounter with the messenger from on high: "take their photographs: sign the warrant for their arrest so they can be handed over to Rojas Agüero": "and you're going to do it?": "yes, I've got no choice, Chaves: I can't say no without tipping someone off, without them smelling a rat: but I'm not letting them have the photos": "so what do you intend doing?" Chaves asked after ordering another drink: "I'll explain in a minute: let's move to that table at the back": finally Chaves went out into the street: Triste waited another quarter of an hour before paying and leaving, taking the camera with him: he ambled down the street till he got to a bus stop where he could catch a bus to the centre: he got into the first bus that came, bought a ticket and spent the journey working out how best to ensure his failure, at the least personal cost

at half past seven he was standing at the foot of the steps to the Congress Building: a sea of demonstrators took up every available inch of space, filling the air with the clamour of voices: he spotted Chaves perched on one of the top steps, possibly the second from the top: and he spotted something else he was looking for: a group of young people sitting down taking a rest, their huge banners rolled up: they belonged to the Peronist Youth Movement: he sauntered about fifty yards in the other direction and sauntered back, making sure he was still within Chaves' field of vision: he started to walk up to the Young Peronists, aiming his camera ready to shoot: as he approached them, he kept his eye on Chaves through the viewfinder as the latter made his way down the steps towards their rear: by the time he was about ten yards away from them, Chaves had come up close behind them: Triste pressed the trigger and the flashlight made everyone look up at him: it was then that Chaves shouted, "look out, he's a cop and he took your picture: don't let him get away," pointing his finger at Cristóbal: in a matter of twenty seconds two or three of the boys from the seated group were on top of him: he felt them snatch the camera and a searing pain in his right jaw: "take your hands off me, I'm a journalist," and he waved the press card he'd managed to get out of his pocket: "a Peronist, did you say?": "I said a journalist": "we all know what you are ... you're a cop," jeered the boy who had hit him and who now had his knee on his chest, pinning him to the ground while he systematically punched him: "here, you can have your bleeding photos," another boy shouted, throwing the open camera, with the film ripped out, down at his side: "you can count yourself lucky," said the one who was hitting him, "you can count yourself lucky we don't want any trouble today, but I'll remember your face, you motherfucking son of a bitch": and he left him lying on the ground, alone, sustaining the scornful gaze of the hundreds of onlookers: he clambered to his feet, panting, and picked up what was left of the camera; "thanks," he thought, "thanks for not killing me, for not sending me to hospital": Chaves had made himself scarce as soon as he had done his bit as accuser: there were no other photographers in the vicinity who might have recorded the details: clutching the precious remains of his camera, he hobbled painfully southwards down Entre Ríos: when he got to Independencia he went into the Bar Carlos Gardel, made for the gents, splashed some water on his face and, feeling a bit better, came out to order a gin at the bar: here's to my little pal and our meeting at half past ten tonight, he thought as he took his first sip, which made his broken lip smart: here's to my little pal who's not going to get his photos or his candidates for rehabilitation or anything

"they went for me: there were lots of them, I don't know how many, but lots of them," Triste told the man, who stared glumly at the camera as if contemplating the image of his own failure: "I suppose we shall have to report it," he spoke finally: "you're the one who'll have to report it: to whoever commissioned you, presumably: I'm fulfilling my obligations by reporting it to you: I don't know who's higher up the ladder, and I don't want to know either, so we'd best leave it at that: if you want you can come and take a photo of my face tomorrow, in colour, with all the bruises showing: then you'll have your proof and there'll be no more questions asked": "there's no need: anyway there were plenty of other photographers who didn't get into trouble, who'll be handing in their cameras intact and who'll sleep soundly after a good day's work": "sleep soundly after a good day's work?" Cristobal asked senselessly: "but of course, why not? does that surprise you?": "of course not, it doesn't surprise me: it's just that I won't sleep soundly at all: it wasn't only my face they hit": "go and see the doctor tomorrow and get an X-ray": "there's no need: it's not the first beating I've taken, and I know there's nothing broken": "Artola, you don't happen to have a bag, do you?": "a what?": "a bag, a plastic bag, the sort you get given at the supermarket: it's to put the camera in": "ah... a bag... sure, just a minute, there's one in the kitchen": "thanks," said the man when Triste delivered the goods: "will that do?": "fine, the camera fits in nicely; now I'll be off: be seeing you, Señor Artola," and he stretched out his hand: Triste looked him in the eye and found himself feeling sorry for him: he took the hand held out to him, demanding a response: finally he was left on his own: so there were plenty of other photographers, I should have known, and they'll sleep soundly after a good day's work: the bastard: I shouldn't have shaken his hand: and he turned on the shower, patted himself dry, got dressed and went out, muttering under his breath: the bastard

Chapter 22. The General Gives His Life
for His Country

The General was a hated man
yet his statue on horseback still stands:
it's outrageous not because he was cruel
but because he never rode a horse.
J. A. GOYTISOLO, *Public Outrage*

General Perón was loved - don't ask why - by his people: General Perón did ride a horse and sailed a boat and flew a plane: in 1955 he had left the country, the monster he had nurtured, to avoid bloodshed: perhaps he realized he was not worth giving one's life for ("our lives for Perón," his followers would later chant, offering what he had not demanded), perhaps he was happy to take a back seat, watching the inevitable escalation of economic disaster from a distance: eighteen years later, in 1973, everyone, for him or against him, was dreaming of his return: the return of the general who by that time was an equestrian caricature of himself - Perón on his ever-photogenic horse, Perón riding on the back of a younger Perón like a fairytale Prince Charming, wading across the river of war like a mounted St. Christopher riding on the back of a St. Christopher from out of a Rubens painting, having ditched the Christ-child of the legend in its waters: Perón as the symbol of a national reconciliation that never happened, that could not happen because not even he, the prophet of a belated social contract signed by the illiterate classes, could stop or change the course of a history that was being decided behind his back: he returned: someone, in some dingy basement office where gems of propaganda are dreamt up, chose to match the awesome slogan, the dangerously enticing lure of "our lives for Perón", with the posthumous claim that "General Perón had given / gave / was to give (delete as applicable) his life for his country": the reality behind that curious, resounding phrase had nothing to do with the risking of life and limb in any liberation struggle: it was a simple, clinical fact: if Perón had stayed in Spain, under the care of Dr. Puigvert, his life might have been slightly prolonged: by a few months, a year at most: his return, prompted by his stand-in Campora's imprudence in "letting out the rabble", as well as by the need to put an end to the armed groups proliferating within, and on the fringes of, the Peronist Movement's Left Wing - which was not, is not, and should not be equated with "the Left" - through a process of splits that would lead them to exterminate each other, took place at a less than ideal moment, physiologically speaking: it was this fact, this shortening of the lifespan of a man nearing his eightieth birthday, that gave rise to talk of his "having given his life for his country": in any case, at the age of eighty you can only give the remains of a life, an afterthought

the General's statement when his personal doctor asked what he intended doing about the Montoneros - "we'll have to let them kill each other off" - was not entirely practicable: he would have to bring in forces extraneous to the Montoneros' internecine wranglings, would have to commission acts of violence that would sow suspicion and mutual mistrust among the various factions: Triste had the dubious honour of witnessing one of these divisive operations, which inevitably had bloody consequences

Perón died on the first of July 1974: that day Triste and Chaves, who had not been contacted for a job of any kind since 12th September of the previous year, but who nevertheless still went on receiving their regular pay-packets, moved to the shanty town for once and for all: for Chaves, the living conditions that would face him from now on were something of a novelty, despite the gradual adaptation process his partner had insisted on: for Triste the move meant no more than a return to earlier stages of his existence in the south beyond the south not so many years ago: that was his natural habitat, and so he was readily accepted: Chaves benefited from the good relations Triste immediately struck up with their neighbours: they got to their new home with the last of their belongings when everyone was in the throes of commenting on Perón's death, and making ready to attend funeral rites as splendid and packed as those of Evita: the General's corpse was put on display for several days, so the people could give a show of fervent loyalty, but the event bore little resemblance to that of twenty-two years previously: the security arrangements were less secure and more rigorous, if not openly hostile to the visitors: those paying homage to the late Perón included all the members of the opposition, which would have been unthinkable at the time of his first presidency: as they entered the shanty town, Chaves was unexpectedly impressed by what he saw: adult men crying their eyes out without any inhibitions, hungry children filled with a sorrow that seemed to outdo their everyday emotional bleakness, grieving women who had already donned what black items of clothing they had been able to lay their hands on, all this surpassed anything the ex-priest might have imagined: he stood at Triste's side as the latter grasped by the neck the bottle of murky wine offered him by one of the men and took a long swig: instead of returning it to its owner, Triste held the bottle out to Chaves, who intuited that he had to follow suit: it was he who, after taking a drink, returned it to its owner: "thanks, comrade," he was taken aback to find himself saying: the man responded with a would-be welcoming smile, constrained by the tangle of sad emotions overwhelming him: "we'd better dump our things and clear out, Chaves: there's not going to be a soul left here today: they'll all be off to see Perón, and it wouldn't look too good if we were the only ones not going to pay our respects: let's go for a little walkabout and come back tomorrow"

Triste spent the night in a hotel with a prostitute: she woke him up at seven in the morning and said: "get your clothes on: it's time to go": "this early?": "I'm going to join the queue to see Perón, aren't you?" the woman expressed her surprise: "maybe later," Triste reassured her: they left the hotel and he invited her to breakfast: in the bright lights of the café they went into, he noticed her eyes: "what's wrong with you? are you OK? your eyes are all puffy": "while you were asleep, I was crying: I spent the whole night crying: I've stopped crying now because I've run out of tears: but when I see him there, my General, laid out in his coffin, I know I'll burst into tears again": Triste fell silent, thinking, wondering what Chaves was doing right now: "where do you live?" she interrupted: "in Villa de Comunicaciones, near Retiro Station": "and you're not a Peronist?": "I don't know, perhaps I am: my mother was a Peronist and she took me to Evita's lying in state": "and you're not coming to Perón's?": "later maybe": "I'm going": "fine: if we see each other again you can tell me about it": "do you want to see me again?": "yes," Triste confessed: she jotted down a number on a paper napkin: "my phone number: my name's Ester": "I'll call you up one of these days": "any time you like": they kissed goodbye, and he watched her disappear into the distance, bound for the queue where everyone else was: everyone except Triste and the odd eccentric

Chaves got back to the shanty town late the following night: "where've you been?" Triste asked: "I joined the queue: I went to see Perón": "and?": "nothing special: a corpse: I still don't understand, Triste": "and what about the people?": "the same old story, hopelessly duped, surrounded by guys like you and me and not able to put two and two together: know something? I think it's Perón who's been paying us all these years": "of course": "what do you mean, of course,

Triste? you've never said anything of the sort to me: when did you come to that conclusion?": "after what happened at Ezeiza, Chaves: though I should have twigged when Lauro was killed in the Plaza de Mayo: but I was only a kid in those days and I didn't know anything about anything": a long silence which Cristóbal finally broke: "tell me, Chaves, when you were a priest did you know a man by the name of Mujica?": "Carlos Mujica, Father Mujica, yes I knew him, why?": "he's the priest here": "here?": "yes, the priest for the shanty town: there's a church, you know: the Church of San Francisco Solano: I was talking to him today: he's a Peronist too": "why do you say too?": "because it seems everyone's a Peronist": "yes, you're right: everyone: and what kind of a Peronist is he?": "well, he cares about the underdog: my guess is he supports the Montoneros, though he insists he's an orthodox Peronist: and he comes out with things a Montonero wouldn't come out with": "such as?": "he said he was prepared to die but that he wasn't prepared to kill anyone else": "of course, he's a Christian": "no, Chaves, not all Christians are like that: lots of them have joined the guerrillas": "and he's one of them too, Triste: in his own way: because that's what it means to be a guerrilla, isn't it? being prepared to die?": "probably, Chaves; you're probably right"

curiosity led Triste to walk past the church at least once a day: hoping to bump into Father Mujica on his way in or out, hoping to stop and have a chat with him, convinced this was a man who had the answers to many of his questions: a conviction which did nothing to change his position on the sidelines, his sense of alienation from the events of his time - except insofar as they impinged on his life in the form of a bleak, cumulative futility, wrenching him out of his natural inclination to lethargy - in other words, even if Father Mujica, or anyone else, were able to satisfy his doubts, Triste would still go on being sad: there was sadness in the curiosity that led him to walk, again and again, past the parish church: on the 11th July, ten days after Perón's death, nine days after his encounter with the priest, as he was nearing the church building on his now habitual route out of the shanty town's forbidden zone, he saw a green car, a Falcon, with what were probably false number plates, a green Falcon like the ones used by Rojas Agüero's men, pull up barely twenty yards from the church door: he knew instantly what was going to happen, and ducked behind a flimsy wall of breeze blocks: Father Mujica came out of San Francisco Solano two minutes later: three of the car's occupants had got out (the fourth was at the steering wheel) with their weapons - a machine gun, two large-bore pistols - visible for all to see: Mujica was looking down at the ground as he came out and a sinister intuition made him look up and see his assassins seconds before they opened fire: it was all over in less than a minute: Mujica fell to the ground on the flagstones outside the church: Cristóbal later discovered from the press reports that fifteen bullets had entered his body: he didn't go to inspect the corpse: he backed away from his hiding-place and headed for home, as people started to come rushing up to see what had happened: "Chaves," he said as he got back to the shack, "they've killed him": "who is it they've killed now, Triste?": "Mujica, Father Mujica," Triste explained: Chaves stared at him, gulping down his gin: Cristóbal guessed what he was thinking and put it into words for him, "it was bound to happen, wasn't it?" he said: "sure, it was bound to happen," said Chaves

Chapter 23. Sometimes the Montoneros Means Us

Beware the victim despite himself,
the oppressor despite himself
and the man who does not take sides
despite himself!
C. VALLEJO, *Spain, Take This Cup From Me*

the pages of the calendar turned for the whole terrible, bloodstained year of 1975: "even those who don't belong to a party behave as if they were activists in some imaginary party," Sartre had commented with reference to earlier events elsewhere: on the 24th December, General Videla, drawing up his New Year resolutions, announced to Perón's widow and Queen Regent that three months later, on the 24th March, he would depose her: Isabel Perón, the Queen Regent, took the news calmly: Triste and Chaves, who all this time had eluded the security net, took the general's words to be a definitive, brutal warning: if so far they had managed to dodge the police raids and patrols that had become everyday currency in the city, the searches that must have been mounted to track them down once it was clear they were no longer prepared to go on collaborating, whether with Rojas Agüero's barbarous rehabilitation centre, Major Mendoza's photos or Father Balmes' crazed inquisitorial outbursts, now everything could easily change, turn against them, crush them: after the 24th December, mindful of the mantle he had promised himself in three months' time, Videla started to take control of the security forces with the connivance and assent of his peers in all three branches of the Armed Forces, availing himself of an order issued - in writing - by Perón's widow, still nominally President: Triste and Chaves had to act before the 24th March: if they put things off till after that date, they ran the risk of postponing them for ever, quite apart from the increased likelihood of their being caught and handed over to the re-educators, torturers and hired assassins: building work had started some time ago on what were to be the three-hundred-and-forty detention, torture and extermination camps that would operate up and down the country: in one of those centres, there was bound to be a place reserved for them

"our old idea of a kidnap, Triste?": "right, Chaves: but not just something done by the two of us, not an amateur affair by a couple of crooks with no bargaining power, no economic clout, no facilities for holding the victim hostage: if they realize it's a smalltime job, we've had it, Chaves": "so what do you propose?": "we'll use the Montoneros' visiting card": "but when we contact the press and let them know our demands and who we're holding hostage, they'll deny it": "and nobody will believe them: all we need say is that we're a splinter group, not officially recognized by the leadership: but we've got arms, cash and the necessary infrastructure: we took a section of the organization with us": "but if they get us after that, it'll be much worse than if they'd got us on our own account": "sure, Chaves: but it'll be harder for them to get us: right now, they've still got to negotiate with a living organization: after a year's systematic persecution, things will be different: there'll be no negotiating: they'll just send in the storm troops and shoot everyone on the spot, or worse": "but now we'll have the Montoneros breathing down our necks too, wanting to know who the hell we are, thinking we're infiltrators trying to set them against one another": "whatever the outcome, it'll be easier to have it out with them than with the military": "are you sure about that, Triste?: you know as well as I do, probably better because you've gone into it, how they operate: just like we used to operate: you get orders to kill someone, seize them and kill them, and you carry out the orders without asking questions:

they didn't set themselves up without help: there must be people behind them we know, the same people who used to hire us: a military command, military discipline, Nazi discipline even": "sure, Chaves, but I'm equally certain there are sectors that have gone it on their own, splinter groups, who they'll pin the blame on: the Montoneros can easily mean us; what's more: sometimes the Montoneros does mean us: individuals who do their own thing and put the Montoneros' signature to it and no one denies or contradicts it, in case they inadvertently tread on each other's toes": "fine: so sometimes the Montoneros means us: when do we start then, Triste?": "tomorrow, at three in the morning"

at half past two, they left the bar in Lacroze where they had something to eat and a couple of drinks: Triste had a bottle of gin wrapped in newspaper tucked under his arm: they walked about eight hundred yards to the garage where the car was kept: every now and then, Triste would go to give it a check, keep it in peak condition, give it a drive round the block: they opened up the door and backed the car out, making as little noise as possible: Cristóbal headed for Barrio Norte and then made for Avenida Alvear: they left the car in a side street and took the bags with the machine guns out of the trunk: they marched to the corner and turned into the avenue: the building they were to enter had a policeman on duty as night porter: Chaves flattened himself against the wall next to the big glass doors: Triste rang the night porter's bell and the latter hauled himself out of the armchair where he was dozing: he came to the door with his pistol trained on Cristóbal, who was standing outside with the bag on the ground beside him and the machine gun tucked behind his back, like a surprise present for a child: when the porter was half a yard away from the door, Triste raised his right hand and showed him a police identification card: the man inside lowered his pistol and went over to the intercom to ask, without opening the bullet-proof glass:

"what do you want?": "Federal Police," Cristóbal lied, "I've come to see Dr. Posse: don't call his apartment: I don't want to give him time to hide anything": the night porter listened and grinned; he'd been expecting something like this for some time now: he'd always thought Posse was up to something: "come in," he said, and pressed the button: Triste kicked the door open and produced the machine gun before the porter had time to raise his pistol again: "drop that revolver," he ordered: Chaves followed him in and they let the door close behind them: Chaves picked up the man's pistol and pocketed it: "down to the garage with you," Triste instructed: the man obeyed: when they got there they made him undress and Chaves donned his uniform: they gagged him and forced him into a sort of broom closet full of old newspapers and empty bottles, which the porters presumably sold off every now and then to make the odd bit on the side: Cristóbal kept his gun trained on the man, sitting gagged on a pile of newspapers, while Chaves loaded a syringe, went up to him and turned his left arm over: he stuck the needle into the vein and pressed the plunger: the effect was virtually instantaneous: the man dropped to the ground like a sack of potatoes: they bound his ankles and wrists, in case the injection wore off unexpectedly, and laid him behind the pile of junk, so he could be seen from the outside: among the keys Triste had taken off him they found the one to the broom closet's metal door: it was half past three: Chaves went upstairs and installed himself in the armchair in the reception area, taking the night porter's place: if anyone came to the door, he was a stand-in, another guard from the same firm: but no one came: he stayed sitting in the armchair till half past five: at that time he made his way back down to the garage

at half past five, Triste had opened up the garage, gone out into the street and driven his own car in, turning it round to face the heavy retractable metal door: Chaves came in through the door from the stairs and found him sitting on the ground facing the elevators, with the machine gun on one side and the bottle on the other: he went over to him and took a long swig of gin: "Dr. Posse goes out at six o'clock sharp," Cristóbal reminded him: at five minutes to six, he got to his feet and picked up the machine gun: Chaves, back in his normal clothes, holding his identical machine gun, took up position with his back to the wall, next to the elevators: anyone coming out would see only Cristóbal: if he proved difficult, Chaves would step in to help: at one minute past six, a red arrow pointing upwards lit up on the indicator: the elevator - the one on the left, next to where Chaves was waiting - stopped at the fourth floor: the downwards arrow lit up a few seconds later: the doors opened to reveal Dr. Posse, who came out and took three steps forward before seeing Triste: at that point he tried to retreat but found the barrel of Chaves' machine gun stuck in his back: the elevator doors closed automatically: "roll up your right sleeve," Triste said: the doctor had his jacket slung over his left arm: Chaves had everything ready: he put his machine gun down and picked up the loaded syringe: he approached Posse from the right, so he would not be in Cristóbal's line of fire should the man try to use him as a shield: "hold your arm out," he ordered: the man knew what was expected of him: Chaves stuck the needle into the vein and pressed down straightaway: he barely had time to pull the needle out before Posse fell to the ground: they bound him hand and foot and gagged him, before loading him into the car trunk: outside it was broad daylight: Triste turned into the first side street and drove off westwards

at midday, from a call box in the full sun, Cristóbal made his first call: to the paper *La Razón*, which came out at half past two, giving time to get the news into that day's edition: "Montoneros," Triste said when the journalist asked who was reporting the kidnap: "two hundred thousand dollars":

"you mean the ransom?": "yes, the ransom": "has an intermediary been named? a relative?": "not yet": the second call was to the doctor's home: "Montoneros," he repeated, ignoring the family's question: they wanted to know how he was: "Dr. Posse is fine: we want two hundred thousand dollars": "where? when?": "you'll be hearing from us": he hung up and went into a bar some thirty yards away: before ten minutes had elapsed, a police car drew up: they'd traced the call: they searched the call box inch by inch in the hope of finding a message: disappointed, they drove off: Triste ordered another gin

"see, Chaves?" he told his partner, over next morning's papers where there was no denial from any quarter, "see how sometimes the Montoneros means us?"

Chapter 24. Underground

Following the line of endless walls
They canter on. The moonlight narrows
The feeble contours of their shadows
And in its glow their colour palls.
LEOPOLDO LUGONES, *Moonstruck Dogs*

Dr. Julio Bravo Posse, apart from being a military doctor and owning a pharmaceutical laboratory, was associate director of, and shareholder in, several companies: the sum of two hundred thousand dollars could easily be raised: all the same it was one of the highest ransoms to have been demanded to date, and both Triste and Chaves knew what that meant: if they got away with it, a lot of cash: but a much more urgent, thorough and painstaking search than if they had put a more modest price on their hostage's head: to avoid payment of such a sum, the concentrated attentions of the security forces would be trained on them for the foreseeable future, so, to get to the talking stage, they would first have to wear down their opponents, dash their hopes only to raise them over and over again, play for time, exhaust their psychological reserves, drive them out of desperation into a private deal behind the backs of the police, the army or whoever

the distance from Posse's apartment to the designated hiding-place was some twelve miles: in the south beyond the south, in an area Triste knew well and where he was well known, well enough at least for people to think of him as Rosario Artola's son, which was sufficient guarantee that anything he was involved in must be "OK by us", he had some time ago rented a tumble-down house, one of those old buildings typical of the province of Buenos Aires, covered with permanently peeling painted clapboards, and with a rusty corrugated iron roof: he had rented it, alleging an irrepressible urge to return to those parts, to the scene of his childhood, when he came across something out of the ordinary in the house: a cellar, with solid earth walls and floor, considerably smaller but otherwise much like the one where he had once taken Pedro Eugenio Aramburu's body to be buried: Triste had gone from Avenida Alvear, by a roundabout route, to the garage near Lacroze where he kept his car: they drove in with Posse in the trunk, and settled down to while away the day as best they could: they had food, drink, cigarettes and a pack of cards to keep them going: they put their hostage on the ground and, every six hours, Chaves gave him another intravenous dose of tranquillisers to keep him unconscious: at two in the morning, they bundled him back into the car, after one last injection: but instead of putting him in the trunk they sat him on the back seat: it took them an hour to get to Triste's house in that godforsaken zone beyond the city's limits, where no one would ask questions if he turned up with some friends, somewhat the worse for drink: they got Posse out of the car and took him straight down to the cellar, which was ready equipped with mattress, chamberpot, a small table to eat off, plus a calendar so he wouldn't lose track of the date: anyway he had a digital watch that gave the date as well as the time, which they let him keep: what Triste forced him to part with was his wedding ring, intending to post it to his wife as a preliminary wordless message that would arouse the wildest speculations among the family: they would be at each other's throats, utterly fed up with their fruitless discussions and petty hatreds when, a week later, they received a photograph showing the hostage with the previous day's newspaper: it was a long drawn out process, easier to get into than to get out of: January was taken up with a succession of messages, some more cryptic and alarming than others, in each case repeating the sum demanded, whether by phone, letter or on the back of a photo of Bravo Posse, but never specifying the arrangements for payment, or the terms, or whether the military doctor would be released immediately: in early February, Triste started to talk of the need to have the money ready: "we've got the money: we want Dr. Bravo Posse," a booming patrician voice said three days after he had first broached the subject: "good: tomorrow you'll get instructions," Cristóbal replied

a man with a blue suit and red tie, with a black briefcase containing the money, was to wait at the intersection of Córdoba and Pueyrredón, on the north-eastern corner, for a car to go past from which someone would signal to him: he was to be reading a copy of *Siete Días*, with reading glasses on: Triste passed the man at three minutes to four: the agreed time was four o'clock: he spotted him from the window of the bus he was in, and asked the driver to drop him on the next corner: there he got out and walked back in the opposite direction, going down Pueyrredón in the direction of Santa Fe: he finally got to within thirty yards of the man: it was then that he saw the other two: police or hired guns, he thought, and carried on walking at the same pace past what should have been his contact: when he got to Calle Paraguay, at three minutes past four, he hailed a taxi and got it to take him to Plaza Italia: there he got out, went into a call box, dialled Bravo Posse's number and, when they picked the receiver up, said, "no dirty tricks," and hung up: another taxi took him back to Paraguay and Pueyrredón, where his own car was parked: he headed south

next day, he rang again to warn them they would be receiving written details of another meeting, which the envoy should attend unaccompanied unless he wanted to put Dr. Bravo Posse's life at risk: a second meeting was indeed arranged, for some five days after the last: Triste chose the spot on the waterfront where he had once discussed with Chaves what they were now doing: the river on one side, open ground on the other: the man with the money was to wait with his back to the river, his elbows on the concrete balustrade, the briefcase between his feet, and his hands visible, at five in the afternoon: Triste drove past the spot at the designated time: the Posse family's envoy was in the agreed place, and he saw no sign of anything untoward in the surrounding area: ten minutes later, after a circuitous detour, he drove back in the opposite direction, passing within fifteen yards of the man: everything seemed in order: he drove off to the city centre, left the car in a parking lot and rang from a bar, after downing a gin: "much better today; same time same place tomorrow: if there are no complications, the doctor will be released forty-eight hours after the money's handed over," and he rang off without waiting for a reply, hastily leaving the premises

Chaves spent his days in the locked cellar, looking after their hostage: he gave him his meals - they often ate together - and left him alone for a couple of minutes when he asked for privacy to relieve himself, still keeping an eye on him all the while through the slightly raised trap door to the cellar: at night time he gave him sleeping pills: Chaves slept when Triste got home and took over the vigil: then it would be Triste's turn to rest: they never spoke in front of Bravo Posse: they discussed their affairs when he was asleep: it was all organized: as soon as they'd got the money they'd leave Bravo Posse drugged, put a heavy weight on top of the trap door to his underground cell, and from Ezeiza Airport, bound for Rio de Janeiro, would send a registered letter explaining how to get to the house, and exactly where the hostage was: Triste had even solved the problem of the heavy weight by buying an old safe at an auction

during his long days in captivity, Bravo Posse spoke only

twice: neither he nor his captors had any interest in establishing a dialogue: the first time he addressed Chaves was not so much to ask a question as to confirm a correct supposition: "you're not in this for politics, are you?" he said: "Montoneros," Chaves insisted half-heartedly: the second time he opened his mouth was to ascertain what destiny they had in store for him: "when this is over, when you get the money I mean, you'll kill me, won't you?" he asked, "because you're not worried about letting me see your faces, and I might recognize you later: you're not expecting me to see the light of day again": "you're wrong: we're going to leave you shut in and doped, and we'll issue the necessary instructions for them to find you within forty-eight hours: by then we'll be far away, out of the country," Chaves reassured him: this interchange, full of unnecessary details, took place two days before the day finally assigned for the handover, the second encounter on the waterfront

Triste took the same route as the day before: he drove past in a southerly direction ten minutes before the appointed time: the man with the briefcase was there: at exactly five o'clock he pulled up by him, in the northbound lane: his machine gun was on the seat beside him: he climbed over it and got out of the passenger door: he went up to the man, pistol at the ready: the man picked up the briefcase and handed it to him: an inexplicable hunch, a dark and lucky premonition made him fling himself to the ground immediately after taking the briefcase: he rolled over and over on the ground till he got to the car, whose engine was still running: as his head went down, he caught a glimpse of the round hole silently opening up in the contact's forehead, at exactly the level where the back of his neck had been a split second before: he scrambled into the driving seat and, lowering his head as best he could, slammed down the accelerator: two men fired from the open ground where they must have been lying in wait, but failed to hit the moving car: Triste drove some thirty yards northwards and, picking up the machine gun with his right hand and resting the barrel on the lower edge of the open passenger-seat window, swerved round into the southbound lane, pressing the trigger down as he sped off: one of the killers fell to the ground, his face dripping with blood: the other hurled himself on to the tarmac and escaped injury: this time it really was the beginning of the end: his car could be recognized, he could be recognized: the fight, lost in advance, against time, always too short, was beginning in earnest

he yelled to Chaves from upstairs: his partner lifted up the trap door and came out to see what was going on: "give him a double dose of tranquillisers: we've got to beat it: there was an ambush and I only just got out of it alive": "and the cash?": "in the car, get a move on": Chaves went down into the cellar where he had spent most of the last forty days: Bravo Posse was waiting for him: when he saw him get the syringe out, he smiled, smiled at Chaves: he knew he was saved: "when you wake up, which you won't for at least twelve hours, you can leave: you'll be free": "thank you," said the doctor: as soon as he was unconscious, a few seconds later, Chaves ran upstairs: Triste had got the four machine guns out of their bags, which were thrown on the back seat of the car: he handed one to Chaves: "we'll keep them on our laps all the way: they may come for us any minute now, and I want to put up a fight: I'd rather get shot than be re-educated by Rojas Agüero and that lot": "so would I," said Chaves: they drove off: they were waiting for them just two hundred yards away, at a turning they had to take to get away: three cars were blocking the road, and a row of marksmen were crouching behind them: the first shot shattered the windshield: Triste kept his foot down on the accelerator: he tried to find a way round by swerving to one side, smashing through two dilapidated garden fences: the marksmen kept their guns trained on them but held their

fire: as soon as the car had got past the barricade, two
rounds aimed at the ground burst its tyres: they could go no
further: they wanted them alive

Chapter 25. An Unhelpful Conversation

Now my fear is such
I leap out of myself
looking for a door,
a voice to stay my fall.
P. A. FERNÁNDEZ, *Time of Light*

"so we've gone over to the enemy, have we, Artola?": the interrogator was Peñaloza, the same Peñaloza who years before had gone with Triste and Chaves to the Military Hospital: "Montoneros now, are we?": Triste denied or affirmed nothing: he stayed silent, gazing blankly ahead, wondering what had happened to his partner, whom he had last seen being bundled into a Falcon, like himself: presumably Chaves had had much the same sort of journey as he had: hooded, pushed on to the car floor, his captors' boots and machine-gun butts digging him in the ribs, on the receiving end of an intermittent rain of kicks, spit and abuse: presumably Chaves had, like him, been dragged out of the car only to be hurled to the ground and laid into by a pack of assailants: assailants whose faces he would probably never see: "fucking little Montonero bastard, thought you could get away with it, did you?" and other such pleasantries invariably heralded a well-aimed kick: in the shins, the groin, the jaw, the knee, the elbow, the liver, the belly: time and time again he was left winded and then, two, three, four seconds later, would come another kick in some other part of his body: Triste had no idea how long it had gone on: all he could remember was that Peñaloza, the man now interrogating him, had intervened with the words: "that'll do, lads: that should have softened him up nicely; take him inside, to the white room": and his assailants had obeyed, pulling him to his feet and helping him hobble to the room indicated by their superior: once they were on their own, Peñaloza took the black sack off his head: "they've made a nice mess of your face," was his first comment: there were no mirrors, for they were in a prison: Triste would never see his own face again: "Chaves says it was a private job, just the two of you, what the hell does he expect us to believe? that you've got no connection with them? you always were a Peronist, weren't you?": "wouldn't be surprised...": Peñaloza slapped him squarely in the jaw: "trying to be clever, are you? what do you mean, wouldn't be surprised?": "I mean I wouldn't be surprised if I'd always been a Peronist, but if so I never realized till now": "and now you have realized?": "wouldn't be surprised...": "all right, Triste, I'm through with you, but make sure you give the boys with the machine the right answers, because they don't have a lot of patience, OK?"

the machine: harnessed to the white table by the same straps he had seen in Rojas Agüero's rehabilitation centre, in the middle of the antiseptic tiled room: "that's for electric torture, Señor Artola: like to have a go?" had been the naval officer's invitation on that previous occasion: and now it was his turn to be experimented on: electric shocks in the gums, the penis, the anus, the thighs, the armpits, continuously, without respite, for three, four hours: each time he passed out they would throw a bucket of cold water over his face and one of the torturers, most likely a doctor, would come and give him a quick check up: and they would take it in turns to interrogate him, asking the same obsessive questions over and over again: his name, their names, how did the Montoneros recruit you, someone must have recruited you, you must have known someone, who ordered the kidnap, your contact's name, the name of the person who recruited you, his name, their names: if he'd known any names, he'd probably have given them: the treatment he was subjected to was ferocious: three or four hours of electric shocks, an incalculable length of time with his head submerged in the tank, forced to swallow the sea of excrement, his nostrils filling with a stench that he would never be able to rid himself of, back for more electric shocks, on with the hood and a dousing down with a hosepipe, fully clothed, before being led off to a freezing underground cell to take a rest, chained hand and foot: there was not enough space to stand up or lie down on the concrete floor: the chains round his wrists and ankles were fixed to the ring cemented into the wall, which also made it impossible to stand up or lie down properly: all one could do was sit with one's back to the clammy wall, one's knees tucked under one's chin and one's arms clasped round them, a position that after a while became intolerable: the rest periods - as they were called - were relatively short: twenty minutes maybe, thirty at the most: Triste felt a genuine sense of relief each time he was brought out, despite knowing he was being released only in order to undergo a further bout of torture: each time his resistance nearly gave out, they would take the hood off and leave him tied to a chair in the middle of a room with dazzling white-tiled walls, floor and ceiling, with powerful overhead spotlights trained in all directions: every now and then, every five or ten minutes (there was no way of knowing), someone would stick his head round the door and shout: "Artola!": "yes," Triste would answer: "keep awake": "I am awake": at one point he thought he recognized Rojas Agüero's voice calling his name: "yes," he said: "not asleep, are you?" the voice threatened: "how could I fall asleep? I'm being re-educated": the joke was not appreciated: the voice's owner burst into the room and knocked him to the ground together with the chair to which he was tied: it wasn't Rojas Agüero, it was some other brute wielding a truncheon or some such instrument with which he proceeded to thrash every inch of Cristóbal's body: the punishment was horrendous, but at least it woke the prisoner up, left lying on his side, chair and all: "bloody bastard," the guard growled as he went out of the door, "even thinks it's funny": the first stage of his time in hell lasted for roughly two weeks, during which Triste ate practically nothing, and what he did eat he threw up with the electric shocks: one day they herded him up some unfamiliar steps: he found himself in a corridor with a row of doors on either side, plain metal doors with just a peephole, too high for the occupant to see out but allowing him to be seen from the outside with the aid of a footstool, and a kind of cat flap at ground level through which food was presumably passed to the prisoner inside: his cell was the last on the right: inside was a rough wooden bunk with no mattress of any kind, and a hole for basic physical needs: there was no chain or flush: Triste would soon discover it was automatically regulated: once an hour, day and night, without fail, water would come thundering down a pipe: all the holes were flushed simultaneously: they gave him a blanket and pushed him in: now he'd have a chance to recover, Cristóbal thought, a chance to replenish his energies so he could go on resisting, go on refusing to talk: as if refusing to talk were difficult for him, when the only name he had to give was that of Chaves: they left him in the cell, with two rolls and two plates of greyish soup for his daily rations: for the first two days he threw up everything he ate: the third day he managed to keep his food down: for the remaining five days he ate everything he was given

then the whole process had to be gone through all over again: torture, beatings to the point of unconsciousness, interrogations, more torture, and back to his cell: but when they pushed him into the cell for the second time, he was in an altogether different state from the first: he could hardly stand, his teeth were chattering and he had lost all sense of time: he managed to wrap the blanket round him, and settled himself on the bunk to sleep: he dreamt of his mother at Evita's lying in state, old Lauro on the tarmac in the Plaza de Mayo, Malena: as if at the movies, he saw them do to Chaves the things they had done to him: he saw Chaves strapped down on the white table and the man systematically applying electric shocks to his body, selecting the organs to be treated with technical precision and expertise: he saw Chaves with his head held down in the tank, in the excrement, by the same men who had finished off Rojas Agüero's prisoner: he woke up with a start just as he was dreaming of Bravo Posse's face at the moment of execution: someone, possibly himself, was pumping bullets into him with a machine gun and he watched him keel over backwards, in slow motion, as blood started to spurt out of the holes in his face and neck: he sat up on the edge of the bunk, feeling an urge to think things out, to do what he had refused to do since his arrest, in an attempt to stave off the collapse he was sure would be the result of thinking: it was the end: did he have to go through all this agony in order to die? it was true he had not been a good man: he had stolen, he had killed, he had committed almost every crime in the book, had violated all God's commandments: but he also knew himself to be the victim of other men whose crimes were worse, much worse than his, men whose crimes were more sophisticated, who were breaking new ground, scaling new heights in the conquest of hitherto undreamt-of crimes: he thought of hypothetical new commandments: "thou shalt not torture", "thou shalt not reduce thy neighbour to an empty shell, slowly draining him of life, thou shalt not reduce him to a bleeding pulp": "thou shalt not drown thy neighbour in large vats of excrement": "thou shalt not string thy neighbour up by the wrists for seven days": "thou shalt not cut off thy neighbour's hands": "thou shalt not mutilate thy neighbour's body": it was another stage in the evolution of sin, in the forward march to the final holocaust: sin was the path that led to annihilation: was there a theological explanation for the hell and annihilation he had come to know? it was true that Triste had not been a good man, but experience had taught him there were others who were unimaginably worse: he remembered Lauro's dying assurance that he owed no one anything, that magically and irreversibly his death cancelled out all Cristóbal's debts: he remembered Manuel Lema in the yard of Devoto Jail saying "I'm not your father": it was then, with his father's repudiation still ringing in his ears, that he saw him, standing in the narrow cell, with the black trousers and impeccable white shirt with rolled-up sleeves he wore on big occasions to address the nation: Perón was standing there, looking at him, waiting for him to notice his presence: Triste clambered to his feet and Perón gestured to him that there was no need, he could sit down again: "we do not favour," he started to recite for Triste's benefit, "the worker at the expense of healthy capital investment, nor big business at the expense of the working classes, but we favour solutions that are of benefit to workers, business and industry alike, because our only interest is the good of the Nation": he fell silent and went on staring at Cristóbal, who was listening open-mouthed: "I'm about to die and you come out with a speech: I don't get it": "I want you to know what you're going to die for," he explained before proceeding: "class divisions," a pause gave the impression he was thinking his speech out as he went along, "class divisions were created to stir up class conflict, but class conflict means the destruction of values": "what values?" Triste inquired: "tradition, property, the family," the dead general expounded: "isn't class conflict responsible for my destruction?" Cristóbal wondered out loud: "possibly, possibly: they've got it in for you because you're a Peronist": "no one knows better than you that I was never a Peronist": "of course I know that, that's why I've come: to impart the doctrine of the cause you never espoused, you never knew": "you've said quite enough with what you've said already, General: I understand your position perfectly, and I can assure you it's not mine": "you're not a communist, are you?" Perón hesitated: "who knows: maybe that's what it's all about," Triste asserted defiantly: "but you're going to die for me: our lives for Perón, even though you refused to collaborate in the purification of the Movement at Ezeiza": "sorry, old ghost, but you've got it all wrong: I'm not going to die for you: they may do me in on your account, but as far as I'm concerned I'm going to die for myself: no one's going to be redeemed by my death, least of all a general": "pride is a terrible sin," Perón accused: "it's not pride, General: I know myself, and it doesn't take a genius to see through you: I'm going to die for myself": "and what about history?" Perón wanted to know: "my dear General," came Triste's whisper, "why don't you go stick history up your arse? just vanish, disappear into thin air, I never want to set eyes on you again": the paternalistic spectre obliged, leaving Cristóbal to his own devices: Perón, he thought, that's just what I needed: before he fell asleep again, he felt an urge to know what had happened to Chaves

Chapter 26. Triste Meets His End

we/ the poor forced to eat patience/
sprouted souls to fly/ wings/ weapons/
against the darkness that lays down its law
of lead/ silence/ suffering/ seclusion/ that is how

we came to take up our souls in combat/ our
wings that knew how to tread on air/
and the least of it was dying/ like a burst of fire
wiping out the mass defeat
JUAN GELMAN, *We The Poor*

although he was unaware of the fact, having at some now
forgotten point lost track of the passing days, it was on the
morning of the 23rd March, in that same fateful year of 1976,
that he was taken out of the cell and transferred to the big
cage in the middle of the compound: it was his first overall
glimpse of the camp, the three-storey building from which he
had just emerged, the grey Nissen huts with barred windows,
the barbed wire, the guards with their weapons trained on
the outside world: they opened the cage door and ordered
him in: "into the madhouse with you, Artola: this is where
we put the ones who couldn't take it, the ones who went off
their hinges rather than talk: you've not cracked up
completely yet: you may have conversations with Perón and
all that, but you've still got some of your wits about you: not
for much longer though": as the day wore on, he realized
what the guard who had brought him there meant: the
stench was unbearable: no one was let out to go to a latrine,
all their bodily functions had to be satisfied inside the metal
cage: at noon, some men appeared with two big pots of food:
one unlocked the door and the other tipped the food on the
ground inside the cage, first one pot and then the other, on
top of the rotting remains of the previous day's food: the
occupants squealed with excitement and hurled themselves

on the putrid scraps: the same men who had brought the food came back with two buckets of water: they all scrabbled to dip their heads in to snatch a drink, it was their one chance of the day: the midday sun beat down remorselessly till well into the afternoon: Triste's fellow inmates were snoring spread-eagled in whatever space they could find: no one spoke: it wasn't just that no one had spoken to him, no one spoke to anyone: at dusk, a man in uniform appeared in the same entrance to the main building through which Triste had passed that morning: he strode forward purposefully and clapped his hands to attract the attention of everyone in the yard: "attention please, gentlemen, we're about to put on a little show for you": they all scrambled to the side of the cage where the master of ceremonies stood and pressed themselves against the bars: a minute later two men came out with a table and chair which they set down a few yards away from the cage: they went back in and came out into the yard with a young man, prematurely bald and in a skeletal condition, whose body was horribly bruised: they had to drag him along the ground because he did not have the strength to walk: they tied him to the chair with a long rope, winding it round and round his torso up to his armpits, leaving his arms hanging free: that part of the operation concluded, they drew the table up in front of him and, with a thick nylon cord, tied his forearms firmly down on its surface: at this point two more men in uniform joined the others: one of them made a speech: "the pitiful specimen you see here was a subversive and a writer: since he has persistently refused any kind of rehabilitation, we propose to make an example of him: may his punishment serve as a warning to future generations": as the officer pontificated, Triste looked at the bound man, who was just in front of him: they had positioned him so he was facing the cage: when his eyes met Cristóbal's, he smiled: Triste smiled back: the officer who had come into the yard with the gruesome speech-maker disappeared for a few seconds and made his re-entry wielding a massive axe: he walked straight up to the table and, with two sure swings, severed the hands of the man who in the world outside had been a writer: two spurts of blood came gushing out of the victim's wrists: Triste's face, still smiling, fell and they all looked on as the man lost consciousness, never again to regain it: Cristóbal rushed to the other side of the cage and started to howl in anger and pity: then, in a loud, clear voice, he recited the Lord's Prayer for all of them to hear: some of his fellow prisoners fell to their knees and started to pray with him, in a hushed murmur: no one was looking when the men in uniform removed what was now a corpse

the next day was the 24th March: Triste, who had spent the whole night awake, sensed that something out of the ordinary was afoot: and effectively, halfway through the morning, the previous evening's master of ceremonies reappeared and read out a proclamation: "attention please, those of you in the cage: at this very moment General Jorge Rafael Videla is assuming office as President of the Republic: this means that the time of leniency is over: you are all to prepare yourselves spiritually for death, because in an hour's time you will be shot: except for Cristóbal Artola, whom our military leaders, in their proverbial bounty, have decided to grant a second chance": Cristóbal would rather have been shot with the rest of them: a second chance meant more torture and there was no way he could give in: he'd told the truth from the start: he had nothing to give them: the hour went by and nothing happened, but eventually the yard filled with officers: it was to be an execution with a difference: one of the officers came over to the monstrous prison and shouted "Artola!": Triste stepped forward: "outside," the officer ordered, unlocking the cage door: as he stepped past the man, he smelt the alcohol on his breath: he looked round at the executioners again and realized this was the novelty, the difference: they were all blind drunk:

"stand over there," directed the officer who had let him out, "while we do our duty": "Rupérez, Valdivia, Aliberti," he proceeded to command, "stand to arms: the rest of you: clear the yard": in a matter of seconds almost all of them had disappeared, leaving Rupérez, Valdivia, Aliberti and their machine guns about half a yard away from the cage: "those of you in the cage," the commanding officer barked, "all together in the middle": the occupants of the cage shuffled into the centre: they were staring at the ground, trying to avoid looking at what was the other side of the bars: they formed a circle with their backs to one another: the three junior officers took two steps forward and inserted the barrels of their machine guns through the bars, to avoid the risk of a bullet ricocheting back at them: "fire!" the commanding officer shouted, suppressing a burp: dozens, hundreds, perhaps thousands of bullets hurtled through the air: Triste saw the pile of human flesh in the middle of the cage turn red with blood and slowly subside in a log-jam of falling bodies: by the time the noise of machine-gun fire had stopped, the pile was almost flat and rivulets of blood were trickling out of the cage in search of fresh air

as Triste came in through the door of the hut where he was taken after the mass execution, he heard the sound of laughter for the first time since he had been in that place: the man laughing was Dr. Bravo Posse: "leave the door open, Triste," he said, "it's hot in here; like a drink?": "yes": "help yourself": when Cristóbal had finished pouring himself a whisky, Bravo Posse proposed a toast: "to General Videla," he said: "to General Videla," echoed the officer next to him: Triste said nothing and knocked back the drink before anyone changed his mind: "there's a friend of yours over there," the doctor said, pointing to a corner of the room: there, lying on a camp-bed stained with blood and urine, was Chaves: Triste went over to him and cupped his left hand round that of his friend: in a barely audible whisper

Chaves notified him: "I'm done for, Triste: I haven't got an unbroken bone left in my body": "Señor Chaves," Bravo Posse interrupted, "has indeed been given special treatment, in addition to the treatment you've received yourself: right now an X-ray would reveal his body to have something like fifty to sixty fractures, not to mention others that might not show up: apart from which certain fractures - in his ribs, for example - are bound to have affected some of his internal organs: Señor Chaves, who can't move an inch even to commit suicide, has for the last three days been begging all and sundry to kill him": "is that right, Chaves? do you want to die?" Cristóbal asked: "yes, Triste: I can't take any more: please": "since today is a great day for the nation and my comrades-in-arms have given me total jurisdiction over the two of you, I had the idea of making you a little proposition: you, Triste, can save us a bit of work by satisfying Chaves' request; in return, I'll get you transferred to a civilian jail, Villa Devoto for example, and one day, in ten to fifteen years' time, say, you may even be a free man: how does that sound to you?": Triste turned to look at Chaves: "say yes, Cristóbal, kill me, please": tears were in his eyes: "give me a gun," Cristóbal asked: Bravo Posse handed him a pistol: he and Chaves looked into each other's eyes as he put the gun to his friend's temple: "bye, Triste": "bye, Chaves": he pressed the trigger and watched as Chaves' face muscles relaxed in death, then he raised the gun to his own temple and pressed the trigger again: nothing happened: "I'd thought of that, Triste, and I only put one bullet in," Bravo Posse declaimed melodramatically: Triste dropped the pistol thinking, bastard, why didn't I kill you when I had you in the cellar? "bastard," he spat at the doctor, and at the officer: "bastard": and he started to run, ran out of the open hut door, ran and ran: " *Viva* Perón, godammit!" he had time to shout before the guards' first round of bullets cut him down: and then, before the second round of bullets silenced him forever, tottering, with one last effort, he shouted "*Patria o*

Muerte! " : "*Patria o Muerte!* " he murmured as he lay crumpled on the ground, wondering what had made him shout that of all things: "*Patria o Muerte!* ": no one heard him

Barcelona, 22 December 1984

Tentative Cautionary Epilogue
in the Form of Readings and Queries

First reading:

we have to start the fight again/ we know
the enemy and we have to start again/
we have to right aberrations of the heart/
regrets/ losses/ so many loved comrades

JUAN GELMAN, *Waiting*, from *If Gently*, published in
exile in Rome, January-March 1980

(but who has to start the fight again? what fight? who has to
start again? who has to right whose aberrations of the heart?
who is this collective voice that speaks? who is this "we"? if
we are no longer a collective voice, who are we? who has to
start again?)

Second reading:

                              can anyone
sleep secure in the knowledge of final victory?

JUAN GELMAN, *Refuges*, from *Acts and Chronicles*,
Buenos Aires, 1971-1973

(but can anyone sleep? is there such a thing as final victory?
who has to start again? what victory?)